I0700970

Praise for "The Warrior Retreat"

A brutally violent tale of war and its consequences.

Duncan Ralston - Author of Woom

Bloody, vicious, but above all, rooted in humanity

Brennan LaFaro - Author of Noose

This story is a page turner and I couldn't put it down.

Brian G. Berry - Author of The Abominable Snowman

WOE TO THOSE WHO DWELL ON EARTH

Horror Stories

JOHN LYNCH

Copyright © 2023 by John Lynch

Original stories Edited by Patrick C. Harrison III

Cover by: Lynne Hansen

All rights reserved.

No part of this book may be reproduced in any form or by any electronic or mechanical means, including information storage and retrieval systems, without written permission from the author, except for the use of brief quotations in a book review.

Cock-Meat sandwich originally published as "G is for Gary Gilroy" in ABC's of Terror Vol 4. From D&T publishing

Stasis originally published in Midnight from beyond the stars from Silver Shamrock Publishing

Noose originally published in Paranormal Contact from Cemetery Gates Media

Blood in the Sand originally published in We are Providence: Tales from the Ocean State from Weird House Press.

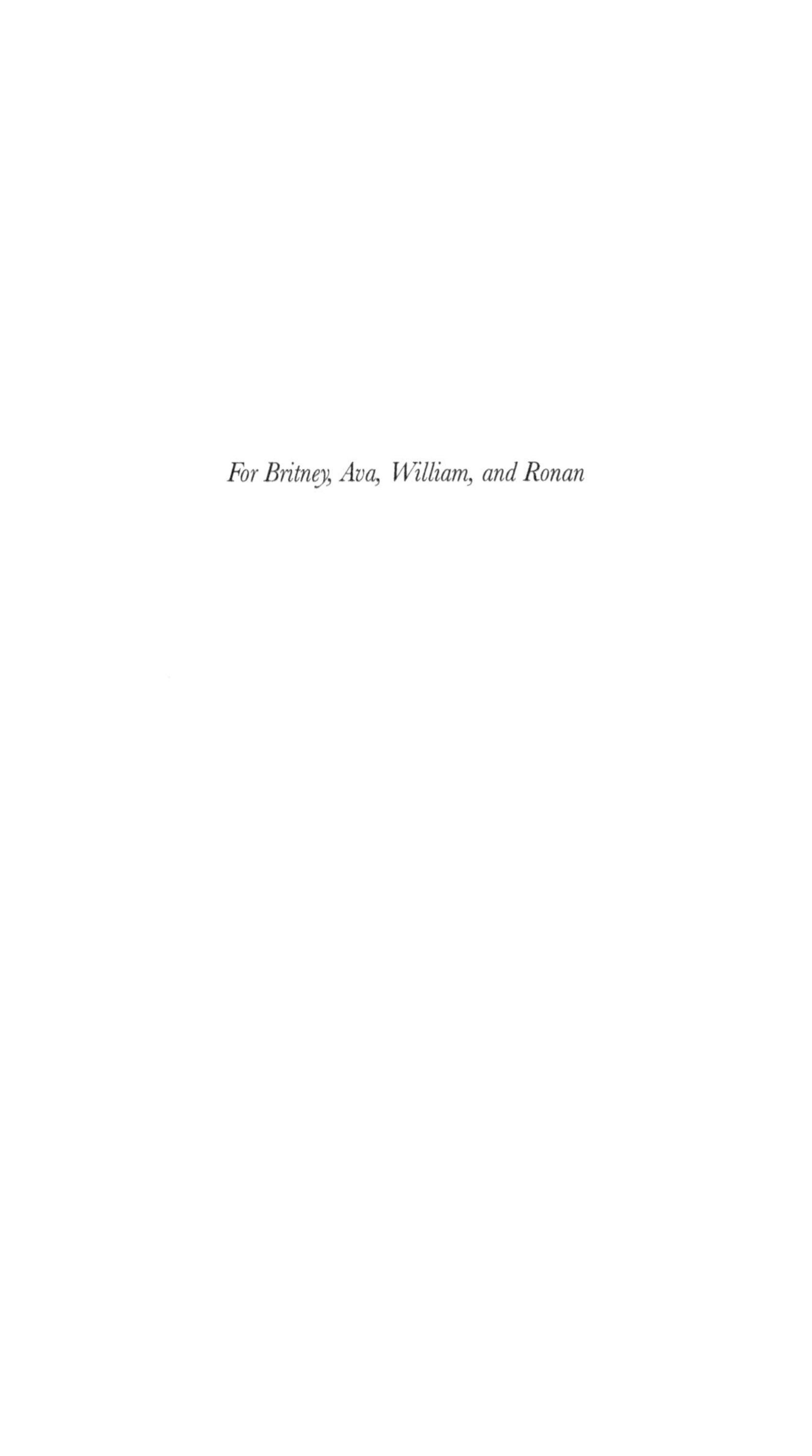

For Britney, Ava, William, and Ronan

"We all go a little mad sometimes."

Norman Bates

Contents

Introduction

This collection has been a long time in the making. I originally began work in 2020 before deciding that it would be a better idea to release a collection after I had a novel finished. That novel would eventually become "The Warrior Retreat", and although it took longer than I anticipated, the reception to that book has been wonderful and I know now that making the choice to delay this collection was the right one. With that book in the rearview, I buckled down and finished this one. What you have in your hands is a mixture of stories both previously published and never before seen. Thank you for your support

Blood In The Sand

1 *0 JUL 09 0445 Hours.*
Private First Class Simpson hopped into the passenger seat of the MRAP and slammed the door. Reaching for the radio, he exhaled slowly.

"Whiskey Actual, this is Whiskey One. Over," he said.

"Whiskey One, this is Whiskey Actual. What's your sitrep?" a voice over the radio responded.

"Whiskey Actual, this is PFC. Simpson, requesting immediate fire support on my position. Drones, mortars, whatever the fuck you've got: drop it— danger close— on my position. Over."

"You're coming in broken and unreadable Whiskey One. Repeat. Over."

"I. NEED. FIRE. DANGER CLOSE. EVERYONE IS DEAD. SEND RE…"

The truck's window imploded next to Simpson's head. Shards of glass embedded in his cheek. A piece pierced his eyeball, and a stream of gelatinous ocular fluid oozed down his cheek.

Simpson screamed.

A large hand grasped his throat. Razor-sharp claws dug into his neck, slicing through his skin. The creature yanked its arm back, tearing out Simpson's esophagus. A geyser of blood exploded from the ragged hole in his neck and painted the windshield with a coating of arterial splatter.

———

10 JUL 09 0745 HOURS.

Private First Class Sarver kept the buttstock of his M4A1 against his shoulder. Rifle at the low ready, he scanned left to right. Sarver's squad, 2nd Squad, had been sent on a search and rescue mission. Sometime between 0400 and 0500, 1st Squad had taken enemy fire. They had lost contact with 1st Squad until PFC. Simpson had gotten on the radio and called for a danger close strike.

Off in the distance, something reflected the sun's rays, shimmering. Sarver made his way to the object.

A digital camera.

———

10 JUL 09 0930 HOURS.

The sun beat down on Sergeant Shinohara as he stood outside of Captain Roquemore's quarters. He wiped the sweat from his brow, streaking the dust and grime across his face. It had been days since his last shower. Running water was a luxury Forward Operating Base Cranston did not have. If cleanliness is godliness, the Marines of FOB Cranston had a one-way ticket to hell.

Shinohara slipped his hand inside the tent's entry flap and announced himself to Captain Roquemore. "Sir, 1st Squad is back from patrol. Lieutenant Gonzalez has the report. We…found something. You're going to want to see this, sir."

"Come inside, Sergeant. Engineers got the generator running last night and the air conditioning makes this inferno feel a little more forgiving."

Sergeant Shinohara stepped inside. The cool air danced over his skin. God, it felt good after the last few hours in the sun. Even in the early morning, the temperature could rise quickly. To make matters worse, the trucks blew out nothing but hot air, leaving the Marines with no respite when out on patrol.

"Tell me, Shino, what happened to my Marines? How is it that an entire platoon has vanished outside of a village that has been deserted for months?" Captain Roquemore walked over to the mini fridge and grabbed a can of Coke.

Sergeant Shinohara pulled a Sony Cybershot digital camera from his pocket. "Video footage, sir," Shinohara said. "We didn't find Private First Class Simpson. We didn't find anyone. Nothing but blood, body parts, discarded weapons, and gear. And the camera. Simpson had been using it to film the patrol; had it strapped to his helmet. Sarver found it on the ground outside of a Humvee. It's not pretty, sir, and it leaves as many questions as it answers. We've never seen anything like it."

Shino popped the memory card out of the camera. "Do you mind?" He nodded at the captain's laptop.

"Be my guest, Sergeant."

———

10 JUL 09 0400 Hours.

PFC Simpson sat in the back seat of the MRAP. He didn't like the idea of being a passenger in the lead vehicle —a vehicle that by nature was the most likely to get struck by an IED—but given his status as the junior Marine in the squad, he didn't exactly get much input as to the seating arrangements of the convoy. His company made that pill harder to swallow. Nothing against Corporal Salazar, but the guy did not know when to shut the fuck up.

As if on cue, Salazar grinned and nodded at the camera attached to Simpson's helmet. "That the same one you used to film me fucking your girl, Simpson?"

"Nope, I left that one at your sister's house, Corporal."

From the driver's seat, Lance Corporal Henriques burst out laughing. "You going to let the newjack talk to you like that, Salad Bar?"

Salazar stared at Simpson. "Puto, you're cleaning the truck when we get back."

"Aye, Corporal." Simpson didn't care about menial tasks. Getting under Salazar's skin was worth it. Besides, it could be worse. He could be on shit burning duty.

"Both of you, shut…"

A concussion rocked the truck, cutting off Sergeant Wilson mid-sentence. The IED explosion whipped up a massive cloud of dirt and debris, leaving the vehicle enveloped in a shroud of darkness. Shrapnel tore through the truck's armor. A two-inch piece of metal grazed Simpson's cheek. Blood trickled from the wound.

"What the fuck, Henriques? You know those potholes are IED magnets," Simpson said.

"I know man, I didn't see it until it was too late," replied Henriques. "You guys ok back there?"

"I'm good," Salazar said.

"I'm hit but fine. I'm bleeding. Nothing serious," Simpson said.

"Pahlmann?" Wilson called.

No response.

"Sergeant, he's breathing," Simpson said, "but he's unconscious."

Wilson turned to Simpson. "Get him out of the turret."

Months of training combat scenarios sent Simpson's body into autopilot. He pulled Pahlmann out of the turret as the rest of the Marines in the vehicle stepped out and swept the surrounding area for secondary IEDs. Simpson knew Henriques would remain in the driver's seat in case a situation arose where the vehicle needed to be moved immediately, provided it was still functional after the blast.

He patted Pahlmann down, feeling for blood or any sign of injury obscured by the layers of uniform and gear.

Nothing.

Simpson was relieved he wouldn't have to perform combat lifesaving measures.

"Sergeant, no blood present. The blast knocked him out, but we've got to get the doc over here to check him out. I don't want to move him any more than I already did in case his neck is fucked up."

"Good idea," Wilson said, finishing up the immediate search of the area surrounding the vehicle. "I'm calling in a CASEVAC on the radio, get the doc on the walkie."

"Aye aye, Sergeant."

Simpson spoke into his radio, "Doc, get your ass up to Vic 1, we've got a man down. Possible head or neck injury."

The truck rumbled violently around Simpson. The sounds of multiple explosions followed in quick succession.

One, two, three, four. Simpson counted the blasts.

Incoming mortar shells. This was no movie. You didn't hear a whistle from a mortar before it fucked your world up. You heard a blast—if, and only if—you were lucky enough to be unharmed or unlucky enough that you were hit and survived.

Machine gun staccato filled the air.

Whump Whump Whump. Simpson heard the Mk-19 spit 40mm high explosive rounds. Superior firepower was the name of the game, and Marines *always* had fire superiority.

Tired of waiting for the corpsman to respond, Simpson flung the back door open and surveyed the scene. The land bridge over the river had been destroyed. From mortar fire or the IED, Simpson wasn't sure. Either way, it didn't matter; the result was the same.

They were cut off from the rest of the squad.

Simpson hopped back in the truck to relay what he saw to Sergeant Wilson.

"Fucking piece of shit radios," Wilson said.

Simpson surmised that Wilson had fared no better in raising communications with base than Simpson had trying to get a hold of the doc.

"Sergeant, things aren't looking so hot. The bridge is gone and there is no way to rendezvous with the rest of the squad. Even if we can contact them, they're going to have to drive a few clicks east to get to another crossing before they can head back this way. It's going to take hours before they get here."

"We have to push into the village and hunker down until either the rest of the squad can get to us, or head-quarters sends the Quick Reaction Force out here. I can't get a hold of them, so it's going to be a while of radio silence before they send them out anyway," Wilson said.

"So, what you're saying is we're stuck here and separated in the middle of an ambush?" Henriques asked. "Well, I've got some more bad news for the both of you. The truck is fucked. There is no way it's going anywhere, not without a wrecker."

Sergeant Wilson punched the dashboard. "Fuck."

"You guys hear that?" Salazar asked.

"Hear what?" Henriques replied.

"Exactly. No more incoming, no return fire, and no radio chatter," Salazar chewed his lip. "It doesn't make sense. Toss me the binoculars. Something is up."

Salazar was right. They should have heard *something* from *someone* across the bridge. Even if their radios were down, someone would have shot a flare…done *something* to signal them.

Unless they were dead.

The thought sent a chill up Simpson's spine. It was inconceivable, he knew, and yet he couldn't shake the feeling that something was wrong.

"Jesus Christ," Salazar dropped the binoculars and started walking toward the demolished land bridge. "No fucking way."

"No fucking way, what?" Simpson picked up the binoculars.

Blood on the trucks. Blood in the sand. A headless corpse lay slumped over the bullet-proof glass of the second vehicle's gun turret. Blood poured from the ragged wound, spilling onto the hood of the truck where it pooled and boiled on the super-hot metal. Limbs were strewn about at random, discarded in the sand along with various pieces of gear. A helmet here, night vision goggles there.

The convoy's still-running trucks and illuminated headlights left the grizzly view clear and Simpson no longer wondered if his friends were dead. The image in the binoculars left no doubt about it. What wasn't clear was *how*. And where did the insurgents go?

Wilson hopped out of the truck, motioned for the few remaining Marines to converge on him. "We've got to make a move. We don't know what is wrong with

Pahlmann, and I couldn't raise anyone on the radios. Nobody is on the way."

Simpson put a pinch of Skoal citrus blend in his bottom lip, adjusted it where he wanted it. "What's the plan?"

"If you shut the fuck up and let me finish, you'll know."

"Aye aye, Sergeant."

Wilson continued. "We need overwatch. Henriques, I want you to remain posted in the turret providing fire support. You're going to pull double duty and see if you can get the radio up and running. Overwatch takes precedence. Don't spend too much time on the radio. Pahlmann is going to have to stay in the truck until we clear the village. Pop a flare if there is anything to report. Use your head, don't waste a flare for nothing."

"Yes, Sergeant," Henriques nodded.

"Simpson, Salazar, you two are with me. We're going to head into the village and clear it. It's small, but with just the three of us, it's going to take time."

Simpson snorted and spat a brown stream into the dirt. "What about civilians, Sergeant?"

"There are no civilians here, Simpson. They deserted the village months ago. Anyone here is a threat. Deal with them accordingly."

"Yes, Sergeant."

"Ok, Marines. Take nothing but full combat load. Leave everything else in the truck. Once we secure a bivouac, we will come back for Henriques and Pahlmann and hunker down at the site until reinforcements arrive."

The situation was *FUBAR*. Simpson knew it, but he was a Marine and he would follow orders until he either killed his way out of this or wound up adding his blood to the kaleidoscope of reds already staining the sand. After mulling it over, Simpson decided he didn't care which way it turned out. His only concern was the absolute destruction of whatever killed his brothers.

After staging their gear, Simpson patrolled alongside his makeshift fireteam toward the village, certain of his impending doom. They made their way through the ragged, bombed-out hole in the mud-brick wall.

A few feet further, they came to the first structure. A one-story brick construction with a roof made of wooden beams and an extra layer of woven willow branches to provide stability. Not that it mattered; Simpson knew damn well one well-placed mortar round was going straight through that roof and causing havoc.

Wilson raised his fist in the air, the signal to halt. "Ok, Marines. This is it. Salazar, you take point. Simpson will be second in the stack. I'll bring up the rear. Heads on a swivel and make sure you turn on your night vision. We need to go house to house and clear every room. Intel on the village suggests we're walking into a ghost town. Considering we just drove into an ambush, we know that's a crock of shit. Kill anything that moves. All friendlies have long since vacated the area," Wilson took a swig of water from the hose hanging over his shoulder. "Take your positions. We move at Salazar's ready."

SALAZAR KICKED THE DOOR INWARD AND FANNED TO THE left, scanning that half. Simpson played off of Salazar and took the right side of the room.

Empty. So far, so good.

"Left side clear," Salazar yelled.

"Right side clear," Simpson screamed.

Adrenaline still coursing through his veins, Simpson took his place behind Salazar in the stack and waited for

Wilson again. Never had Simpson felt more alive than he did when clearing rooms. It was a rush. Something that could never be explained to someone who hadn't done it. If a civilian knew how much he loved it, they would look at him as if he were a monster. *Maybe I am a monster.*

They stormed the room.

Again, the two men took opposing sides of the room.

"Left side cl…" Salazar shouted, gunfire curtailing his voice.

"Right side clear!" Simpson called back. Having cleared his responsibility, he turned toward the gunfire, keeping his rifle at a low ready. Simpson took great caution not to aim at his squad mates.

"Something was there," Salazar said.

"What do you mean?" Wilson crossed the room. "What was there?"

"Something dropped to the floor in front of my face. I couldn't tell what it was. It took a swipe at me and ran off down the hallway. It's gone."

"Jesus, are you hearing yourself, Salazar?"

"Both of you shut the fuck up and take your positions. We're going down the hall. Salazar, calm the fuck down. We don't need you jumping every time you see a shadow," Wilson said.

"Aye aye, Sergeant."

Simpson got behind Salazar once more. The trust he once had in Salazar dwindled. The man wasn't good in a life-or-death situation.

Wilson tapped Simpson.

Simpson hesitated for a moment, tapped Salazar.

Salazar swung around, keeping his rifle trained straight down the hallway. Following Salazar's lead, Simpson swung around the corner, keeping his muzzle aimed to the right of Salazar. Wilson walked backward, keeping his muzzle pointed to the rear.

A noise from the right side of the hallway. Simpson scanned the length of it, taking care to keep his friend out of his line of fire. A shadow scuttled across the wall on the far side of the hall. The green murk of the night vision made it difficult to identify what he had seen. "You see that, Salazar?"

"I don't know what I saw. Whatever it was, it looked like it crawled out of the window."

Wilson took charge. "Keep moving, Marines. Salazar, when we get to the end, you stack on the door. Simpson, you peel off and clear the window, I'll hold the rear. After you clear the window, take the wall opposite Salazar. We're going to flash our way in."

"Aye aye, Sergeant."

The Marines continued down the dark hallway. Simpson peeled off and cleared the window, training his rifle at the topmost, far corner of the wall. As he walked, he scanned down, to the right, and back to the top again.

"Window clear," Simpson took position on the wall opposite Salazar.

Wilson took up the rear once again. "Same order of entry. Simpson, when Salazar gives the go ahead, you toss the flash. Both of you keep your eyes to the rear."

Salazar muttered something to himself, turned to Simpson, and gave a nod.

Keeping his back against the wall and his head toward the front of the hut, Simpson removed the M84 from where it hung on his vest, pulled the pin, and tossed it behind him.

The stun grenade bounced off the floor and rolled further into the room before bursting, creating a bright flash followed by a bang. The sound reverberated through the hall. Simpson's ears rang.

Something hissed from beyond the doorway.

The Marines swung out one after another, each manning their assignment without hesitation. All the hours of training. The blood, sweat, and tears had transformed them into a well-oiled machine.

Salazar double tapped the trigger. Keeping his barrel on the right side of the room, Simpson saw a creature slumped in the corner.

"Left side clear," Salazar shouted.

"Right side clear," Simpson echoed.

"What the fuck is that?" Wilson crossed the room. "Turn your googles off."

Wilson shined a flashlight. The beam landed on a corpse.

It was Henriques. His neck torn to shreds. Blood gushed from the gaping hole between his shoulder and head. A few strands of gristle were the only thing keeping the head attached to the body.

Beyond Henriques, a monstrosity lay sprawled on the floor. Black viscous fluid pooled around the creature's giant, hairless head. Simpson shuddered at the rows of razor-sharp teeth protruding from the gaping mouth. Like something that had never seen the sun a day in its life, its skin was pale, fish-belly white. The flesh was pulled so taut over its muscular body, the veins beneath it seemed as if they would burst from its skin. Its long, muscular arms and legs ended in multi-segmented, finger-like appendages. Each appendage ended in six-inch claws.

Salazar stood over the creature.

Simpson noticed an almost imperceptible rise and fall of its chest. "Salazar, get back!"

The creature exploded up from the floor and swiped at

Salazar's neck. Blood spewed, bathing the creature and the wall behind it in gore.

Simpson raised his weapon and opened fire. Wilson did the same. Both men emptied an entire magazine into the creature before it went down.

A hiss from above.

In one smooth motion, Simpson took a knee, looked up, ejected the spent magazine, and inserted a fresh one. "Wilson, above you!"

The second creature dropped from the ceiling onto Wilson, taking him to the ground and ripping his throat out.

"No!" Simpson yelled and fired a three-round burst at the creature, doing his best to aim as high as possible to avoid shooting Wilson. The creature was faster than anything Simpson had ever seen. Somehow it leaped off of Wilson, avoiding the burst. Simpson fired again, this time single shots. Marines never fired three-round bursts. Simpson felt stupid for having done so earlier.

Despite his best efforts to place well-aimed shots on target, the creature scurried across the wall at an alarming clip, avoiding round after round from Simpson's M4.

"Stay still, fucker!" Simpson double tapped. Both rounds striking the wall wide of the intended target.

The creature stopped. It looked at Simpson and emitted a terrible sound from its hideous, charred face. Wilson's blood still streaked down the burned flesh. Its enormous eyes were nothing but white.

Simpson shuddered.

He collected himself and pulled the trigger.

Click.

How did I not realize the bolt was to the rear? Rookie mistake.

His error may cost him dearly.

Slow is smooth, smooth is fast.

The core tenet of reloading under duress ran through his mind. In one buttery smooth motion, he dropped to a knee and swapped magazines before finally sending the bolt home, all in under three seconds.

It wasn't fast enough.

Despite keeping the buttstock of the weapon in his shoulder and trained on his target the entire time, the creature had leapt off the wall as Simpson was slapping the bolt release home to chamber another round. He fired, but the trajectory of the monster's leap sent it over the round before colliding with Simpson, knocking him flat.

Winded, but running on adrenaline and a newfound appreciation for life, Simpson held his M4 horizontally and pushed out with all the force he could muster. The creature's claws wrapped around the rifle as it craned its neck closer to Simpson's face. It gnashed its teeth, eager to rip and tear chunks of flesh.

I can't keep it off me much longer. It's too strong.

Memories from his past crashed into Simpson's mind, a highlight reel of who he had been before the Marine Corps. Before this monster. Walking the pier with his father at Rocky Point. Eating clam cakes with his brother at Iggy's, the Simpson boys' favorite eatery. Fishing in Narraganset with his son, Ronan.

The thought of Ronan snapped him back to the present, and an idea struck Simpson. What if the creature was sensitive to light? Its skin appeared to have never been subjected to the sun, and the huge white eyes led credence to Simpson's fast-flowing theory that the monster was nocturnal. And hadn't the flashbang slowed the first one down enough that they had actually managed to pump its guts full of lead?

Simpson used one arm to maintain his grip on the rifle —it was the only thing keeping him alive—while he used the other to snatch his tactical flashlight from his shoulder. Simpson pointed it at the creature's eyes and toggled the switch.

It shrieked and let go of the rifle, sitting upright and relieving the pressure from Simpson's chest. He used the momentary respite to grab his Ka-Bar and buried the blade in the creature's neck. He pulled the blade out and plunged it into the creature repeatedly. Its blood spewed like a geyser, coating Simpson.

After one last stab, he sheathed his Ka-Bar and retrieved his rifle from where it had fallen on the ground. Salazar, Henriques, and Wilson were all dead. He had seen no sign of Pahlmann.

I need to get back to the truck. Maybe Henriques had fixed the radio.

Simpson left his night vision switched off and used his flashlight to navigate. He took off running down the hallway and through the main entryway.

A creature screeched from behind him.

Simpson kept running. He was in the home stretch now. Past the village wall and then another fifteen, *maybe* twenty yards and he…

Made it!

Simpson hopped into the passenger seat of the MRAP and slammed the door. Reaching for the radio, he exhaled slowly.

Thank God. Please, please let Henriques have fixed this piece of shit.

10 JUL 09 1015 HOURS.

. . .

CAPTAIN ROQUEMORE WATCHED THE FIRST-PERSON VIEW OF Private Simpson being eviscerated by some kind of monstrosity.

"Not a word of this to anyone, Sergeant. You're dismissed." Captain Roquemore hit the stop button on the device and removed the memory card from within it. When he was sure that the Sergeant had seen himself out, Captain Roquemore made his way to the large gun safe at the other side of his tent, spinning the dial and cracking it open. He placed both the camera and the memory card within, alongside other "discarded" cameras, laptops, rolls of film, and polaroid shots.

Biting his lip, he knew a tough decision was ahead of him. Roquemore closed the safe and flicked the dial. Something would have to be done about Sergeant Shinohara; he couldn't be trusted to keep this quiet. Captain Roquemore saw an urgent mission in Shino's future. One he wouldn't be returning from.

The Butcher of Bridgeport

Caverly endured the long bus ride up the mountainous terrain in relative silence. Well, *he* was silent. His fellow Marines, who were also unlucky enough to embark on this horrifically shitty training operation, were equal parts disgruntled and excited at the opportunity to train in Bridgeport, California, the home of the USMC Mountain Warfare Training Center. Stationed in Hawaii, it was a rare opportunity for the Marines of 2nd Battalion 3rd Marine Division—the so-called *Island Warriors*—to step outside of their comfort zones and engage in some good, old fashioned miserable training. Field operations sucked by design, and Caverly couldn't imagine what special section of Hell he was about to endure.

Fresh out of boot camp, Caverly was the fucking new guy, which was about as fun as dragging your scrotum across a mile of broken glass. The men on this bus took hazing to new heights. Late night workouts in his barracks room, but instead of P.T. gear, he wore a gas mask.

And a fucking tutu.

It was a rite of passage, or at least they told him it was. Either way, there was nothing fun about getting smoked after hours, dressed like the biohazard fairy. All for the viewing pleasure of a few alcoholic Marines. Caverly hoped that those pictures wouldn't end up on social media. That would make getting laid when he went back home on vacation an insurmountable task.

It hadn't been *all* bad. After the tutu incident, the same Marines tried to prank him. One that ended to his benefit. Caverly had pulled barracks duty—a 24-hour post requiring him to look after the living quarters. Sometime after midnight, Lance Corporal Erickson had knocked on his door. He complained of a loud barracks party in the room adjacent to his. Caverly found himself stuck between a rock and a hard place. He could either ignore the complaint, thereby ensuring the Marine he had blown off would pay him a late night visit some time in the not-so-distant future, or, he could investigate the complaint and piss off another senior Marine, thereby ensuring *that* individual would be the one paying him a late night visit.

Looks like I'll be getting the green weenie either way. I'd better check this complaint out, just to be safe. Caverly had put his book down and marched to the room in question. He straightened his uniform tie, and knocked on the door, looking like the world's biggest dickhead. He could feel Erickson staring, and heard him snicker. Nobody answered. Caverly had been about to step off when the door swung open, revealing a tatted-up, muscle-bound Marine.

He was as naked as the day he was born, but his cock was much bigger than it had been at birth. Glistening and erect, it pointed at Caverly, swaying to and fro. Caverly couldn't help but stare at it. It gave the blue whale a run for its money.

"Yeah?" the Marine asked.

"Umm, there were some noise complaints. I just wanted to ask you if you could keep it down. Some of the Marines have P.T. tomorrow morning."

The Marine shifted in the doorway, giving Caverly a clear line of sight to the woman on the bed. Naked, she was propped on her hands and knees. A ball gag stuffed in her mouth muffled her moans as the Marine behind her pumped away. He either didn't know Caverly was there, or didn't care.

"Sorry, we thought the gag would help," the Marine said. "You want her to shut up, you're welcome to go tell them."

Caverly bit his lip. He didn't want to be a cockblock, but women weren't allowed in the barracks after hours. He had to put a stop to this. "You're right. It's my job, I guess." Caverly approached the couple. "Umm, I got some noise complaints, and this woman can't be here at this time of the night. And nobody signed her in, which is against regulations."

The Marine stopped clapping the young lady's cheeks. His pectoral muscles rippled as he flexed. He was peacocking, trying to impress the woman and intimidate Caverly. The man sighed. "What the fuck did you say to me, boot?"

"She leaves or I'm telling the officer of the day."

"Babygirl, what do you think?" The Marine slapped her ass and she resumed sliding up and down his shaft.

Caverly's face reddened and he looked away. The situation was awkward enough without looking her in the eyes.

She spit the ball out and smiled. "He's kind of cute," she said and reached for Caverly's belt. His cock responded to her advance.

Suddenly he didn't care how awkward the situation felt.

Boom.

The bus struck a pothole, rattling the Marines inside of it, stirring Caverly from his thoughts.

Caverly, back in the present, heard Sergeant Hinther still going on about some old Marine Corps urban legend.

"Whatever is out there, they call it The Butcher, gents. I've been to Bridgeport twice myself, and one thing I can tell you is that people, including Marines, go missing in those mountains. In the past, we've found human remains close to base, and I personally know of four different Marines who have just vanished without a trace. The Corps fed their families a line of bullshit about training accidents. Told the families the bodies were unrecoverable. But I promise you boys, these weren't no accidents. Keep your eyes open and take a battle buddy everywhere," Sergeant Hinther finished. He took a seat, his words leaving the Marines in a stunned silence.

Caverly swallowed the lump in his throat. Was the sergeant nuts? Caverly had heard the rumors. Despite being one of the most decorated Marines in their unit, Sergeant Hinther was also a notorious party animal. Everyone knew it, but his uncanny ability to survive every surprise piss test was just as legendary. Had years of steroid abuse and cocaine fried his brain?

The bus parked and Sergeant Hinther barked orders at his subordinates.

Training had begun the moment the Marines arrived at Bridgeport, and in typical Marine Corps fashion, it sucked. Live fire gun ranges, mountain rappelling, hikes across snow-covered, mountainous terrain, all while outfitted with full combat loads and cold weather gear. Blowing shit up was great, but the cold had sapped the joy from the entire experience. One more night of misery and then they would be on a flight back to Kaneohe Bay, where they would pound beers at the Kailua Pub and laugh at how bad training had sucked. All that was left between Caverly and a night of eating pizza, drinking beers, and getting his dick sucked was one final training exercise—low-light land navigation. It would be a cakewalk with an experienced Marine like Sergeant Hinther in charge.

And it was.

Until the blizzard hit.

The morning weather report had shown no reason to expect anything other than clear skies, so they stepped off much as they would any other training exercise. There had been no reason to expect any…extenuating circumstances.

Caverly was assigned point man, despite being the least experienced navigator in the squad. Sergeant Hinther told him it was imperative to know the jobs of every Marine around you. You never knew when a stray bullet or IED would lead to a combat promotion.

They had set off at sunset, and had been at it for about two hours. Caverly turned around and checked the Marines behind him. He could hardly pick out their silhouettes in the harsh storm. Whipping wind buffeted his face, stinging it with cold and snow.

Focusing, he saw Sergeant Hinther give the signal to halt, and then raised his arm and swung it in horizontal circles. *Assemble on me*, it meant. Caverly doubled back and stood before the sergeant, awaiting further instruction.

"Marines, I'm not gonna bullshit you, I lost communication an hour ago. I let Caverly continue because we were more than halfway complete, and the little fucker had been doing a good job. I thought we could make it, despite the storm. Had we sheltered in place and waited to re-establish communication, we would have been waiting longer for headquarters platoon to send a recovery party for us than it would take us to complete the course. I made the wrong call."

Sergeant Hinther crouched down and placed his hands on his knees. "Headquarters will send a search and rescue party to look for us eventually, but standard operating procedure says that won't happen for at least a few more hours. We need to take shelter. Drop your packs, grab your shovels, and get digging. All hands on deck for this, we need it done yesterday."

Caverly dropped his gear and picked up his shovel. "Do we need an overwatch, Sergeant?"

"Negative, Private. Not sure why you heard 'all hands on deck' and thought your bitch ass could get out of digging the fucking hole. Stop being a bitch, you're not getting out of shoveling. If we don't get out of this storm, we're going to die," Sergeant Hinther said.

Despite the cold weather, the Marines worked up a sweat as they dug their pit. They stopped only to take sips of water. The cold was blistering, but dehydration was still a risk.

Caverly shoveled snow for what felt like days on end. He grew up a military brat himself and had spent most of his younger years in California. Until Bridgeport, he had only seen snow on television. Now, he fought for survival in it. The pressure chipped away at his psyche. Exhausted, hungry, and cold, Caverly threw his shovel down. He crossed his arms, burying his hands in his armpits. "Fuck this shit, man, we're going to die out here."

DePina dropped his shovel and grabbed Caverly by the parka. "You're going to want to pick that up and keep on digging, bitch. Or I'll kill you myself."

"Man, I'm serious, we're fucked. Why are we even out here in this shit?"

"I won't say it again."

"Both of you knock the shit off and keep digging. I'm

not dealing with anyone's shit tonight," Sergeant Hinther ordered.

DePina let go of Caverly and picked his shovel up. Caverly watched in silence as the Marines kept shoveling show. He clenched his teeth and stared at Clark, AKA Walt Disney. He always had some bullshit story to tell. Clark locked eyes with Caverly, smiled, and went back to shoveling snow. Caverly wanted to slap the shit-eating grin off Clark's face. The thought put him in a better mood. He picked his shovel back up and continued digging with the rest of the guys.

Once the pit was dug they erected tents. The job of setting up shelter was far less exhausting and time consuming than digging the pit had been.

Caverly stowed his gear inside his tent, stripped down to his underwear, and crawled in. He zipped it closed and tried to get comfortable. He wasn't happy about sharing a tent with DePina, but it could be worse. He could be stuck in a confined area with Clark.

Caverly rested his head on his helmet, using it as a pillow. Before long, he dozed off.

He dreamed of a warm fire. Of sitting around it, telling stories. Something about a guy named the butcher. A sharp pain in his ribs woke him.

"Get up," DePina said.

"Why did you kick me, dickhead?"

DePina tossed Caverly his boots. "I have to piss. I need a battle buddy. That's you."

"You couldn't do this earlier?"

"Nope. I didn't have to piss. I do now, so get the fuck up, pussy."

Caverly dressed quickly, picked up his rifle, and followed DePina into the storm. They climbed out of the pit and trudged through the snow. Caverly remained close to DePina, not wanting to lose him in the thick storm. Sheets of heavy snow whipped them and stung their faces. Caverly raised his hand to block the elements.

DePina stopped walking and Caverly collided with him, nearly knocking DePina over. DePina turned around and punched Caverly in the chest, sending him sprawling. "Stay there until I get back," he said.

"Asshole," Caverly whispered as he stood.

He shivered. The snow had soaked through his pants. If DePina hadn't rushed him, he would have put on his Gore-Tex trousers.

"Yo, DePina!" he called. "Let's go, man, it's fucking freezing out here."

The wind howled in response.

Caverly turned and walked toward the tent. "Fuck him."

A blood-curdling scream stopped him in his tracks.

Caverly didn't bother turning around to see what caused it. It was the fucking Butcher. What else could it be? The smartest and *safest* thing he could do was get backup. Let the sergeant handle it.

He waded through the snow, thighs burning by the time he made it back. He needed to rest, but DePina's life was at stake, and as much as Caverly thought DePina deserved whatever he had coming, he couldn't *not* get help.

Caverly unzipped Hinther's tent. "Sergeant," he said, "something happened to DePina. He's gone."

Hinther roused from his sleep. "What do you mean he's gone? Where did he go, Marine?"

Caverly explained the situation to Hinther.

"You left him alone, in whiteout conditions, when we don't even have contact with Headquarters? Have you lost your fucking mind?" Hinther started gearing up. "Was Clark with you?"

"Negative, Sergeant. I haven't seen him since we bivouacked."

"Shit. He must have stepped out while I was asleep. Get geared up. Bring your weapon and a full combat load. The storm is the least of our worries."

Caverly's face turned white. He had to be talking about The Butcher. Caverly had hoped the story was just that—a story—but by the looks of things, The Butcher might be as real as he. "Aye-aye, Sergeant."

For the first, and maybe last time, Caverly prepared for battle.

After donning both combat and cold weather gear, Caverly met Hinther outside of his tent.

"You look like a fucking soup sandwich, Marine." Hinther jiggled Caverly's armor. He nodded at Caverly's rifle. "That thing hot?" he asked.

"Aye, Sergeant."

"Then let's get this done," Hinther turned around and trudged through the snow.

Caverly maintained close proximity to Hinther, following in his tracks in order to traverse the snowscape himself. It was far less exhausting to follow someone's path than to make your own. Caverly thought there was a deeper meaning in that, but didn't have time to reflect.

They marched toward DePina's last known position. Caverly grunted, leaned forward, and pulled the straps on his pack tighter, cinching it higher on his body. The relief was instant, and made the load easier to bear. When he looked forward again, Hinther remained in position, but had taken a knee.

"What's up, Sergeant?" Caverly said.

"Come check this out."

Following orders, Caverly peered over Hinther's shoulder. He barely managed to turn his head enough to avoid puking all over Hinther. In his gloved hand, the sergeant turned an eyeball around between his thumb and forefinger. The green shade of the pupil told them the eye had likely belonged to Clark.

"Knock that shit off. The Butcher is here. I fucking told you." Hinther tossed the eyeball in the snow. "I don't tell fairy tales. Clark is missing, probably worse, and so is DePina. That might be the only piece of them we find. You assholes thought I was playing games on the bus, but this is no game. You were here training for a war, and while the fight and the enemy is not the one we thought, you're still a trained warrior. Behave like one."

Tree branches rustled just ahead of them. Caverly looked up. Something sped at him, but through the blinding snow, he didn't see it until it was too late to move. An object collided with his chest before falling to the snow in front of him. It hit him hard, rocking him on his feet, almost sending him flat on his ass.

He looked down and Clark's lifeless eye stared at him, the one-eyed severed head of his brother in arms confirming their earlier suspicion as to the owner of the eyeball. Blood pooled around the ragged stump of what was left of Clark's neck. What could tear a man's head off like that? He shrieked in fear. His foot shot out, an involuntary reaction at the realization of what lie before him, punting the head across the snow.

"Did you fucking see that, Sergeant? Something ripped Clark's fucking head off and threw it at me." Caverly dry heaved.

"Keep your eyes on a swivel, Caverly."

A bestial roar came from the trees. A massive blur raced toward them.

"Shoot the fucker!" Hinther ordered.

Caverly opened fire. A three round burst. The thing cut

to the right and continued straight for them. Caverly fired twice more. One of the rounds punched into The Butcher's shoulder, but it had no effect. In the space of a few seconds, Caverly had spent almost a third of his ammo.

"Conserve your ammo, Caverly," Hinther shouted as he fired well-aimed shots at The Butcher. His aim was true, but the thing took the bullets in stride. The Butcher leaped over their heads, turned around and swiped a massive arm across Hinther's back. He fell face first in the snow.

The Butcher pounced. Hinther, operating on combat instinct, rolled to his left. The Butcher landed in the snow narrowly missing him. Hinther scrambled to his feet. His ballistic insert slid out of a gash in his armor and landed in the snow. The butcher had cleaved it into two pieces.

Caverly opened fire again.

Bloody holes appeared all over the creature's body. Caverly marveled at The Butcher's massive frame. If seen at a distance, it could be mistaken for a large, deformed man. Up close, its long arms ending in blade-like appendages betrayed that facade. The creature's large black eyes rested above gaunt cheekbones. The Butcher hissed at them. Rows of razor-sharp teeth clacked together. Blood trickled down its chin, running down its naked, alabaster skin. Large muscles rippled beneath its skin as it flexed. The creature's cock dangled comically between its legs; it was naked as the day Hell birthed it. Arms akimbo, The Butcher looked to the sky and howled into the storm.

He squeezed the trigger, but it was no use. In the frenzy of action, Caverly had run out of ammo, the bolt locking to the rear. He had made a rookie error, not paying attention to his weapon in combat.

Ignoring the snowy terrain, he dropped to one knee, using his right hand to eject the spent magazine as his left hand grabbed a new one. He smacked it into the magazine well. The muzzle of his M4 remained trained on The Butcher as he slapped the bolt release, chambering a round. The process took less than two seconds. Caverly flipped the fire selector from burst to single and fired three well-aimed shots in quick succession.

One of the rounds found The Butcher's left eye, the other two penetrated his chest. Ocular fluid ran down its cheek. Pissed off, it charged Caverly.

Hinther threw his rifle into the snow and ran at The Butcher, intercepting the creature before it reached Caverly. The force sent both man and beast sprawling to the snow. The tangle of bodies left Caverly with no clear shot.

Hinther sat atop The Butcher and pulled his sidearm from his leg holster. He jammed it in the creature's mouth. The Butcher bit down, its razor teeth shearing the Beretta into two pieces. The creature arced its blade-like hand up and buried it inside Hinther's skull. Blood and brain erupted from Hinther's head, splattering across the monster.

Caverly's jaw dropped. A decorated Marine killed in combat while attempting to save his life.

The Butcher shook its arm, trying to break loose, but its bladed hand remained lodged in Hinther's skull.

Caverly squeezed the trigger again. The rifle failed to fire once again, this time no fault of Caverly's. M4's were notoriously unreliable, and his jammed in the heat of battle.

"No!" Caverly screamed. He threw his rifle down and made a break for Hinther's M4. It had an M203 grenade launcher attachment. Hopefully Hinther had loaded it. If not, he would see his squad in Valhalla.

Caverly snatched the weapon from the snow, placed the

buttstock in the hollow of his shoulder and aimed it at The Butcher.

"One ugly motherfucker," Caverly said, praying as he squeezed the trigger.

Thwoomp.

A grenade launched from the tube. Caverly's aim was spot on. The round hit The Butcher's chest, exploding on contact. Blood, shrapnel, and flesh rained from the sky. Caverly stared at the gory mist, hoping it was over. When it cleared, he exhaled a breath he hadn't known he was holding.

The rifle fell out of Caverly's hands, discarded like trash, the weapon was of no further use to him. The trauma of the evening's hellacious experience left him numb, and he no longer cared what would happen to him if the rest of his unit sent a rescue team to find them, only to find his weapon was missing. Fuck, men were dead. His whole fire team, dead in minutes.

He trudged through the deep powder and stopped at what remained of Hinther and The Butcher. The storm continued to rage around Caverly, even as the one within him threatened to push him over the edge. He sifted through the viscera, moving bits and pieces of internal organs and unidentified organic tissue. Caverly searched the entrails until he discovered what he was looking for—Hinther's dog tags. He dropped to his knees as the sobs racked his body, but there was no time for grieving. The reality of the situation was simple—he had survived The Butcher, but he still had to grit out the storm.

The shelter they had erected earlier was his only hope.

———

Pressing the quick release shoulder clips, Caverly's body armor fell to the ground. It felt good to drop that burden. The gear was heavy under optimal conditions, but saturated with snow, water, and blood, it was damn near unbearable. He stripped off the wet layers of clothing and stashed them in between the tent's inner and outer layers. Nude, he crawled through the opening and zipped the entrance behind him shut. His teeth chattered, and he rubbed his arms, willing his body to create the smallest bit of warmth. Caverly wrapped himself in his sleeping bag and hunkered in the corner. His knuckles turned white as he held his Ka-Bar knife in a death grip, waiting for a search and rescue team to arrive.

A howl ripped through the blizzard.

And another.

Caverly counted five of them, distinct shrieks. Communicating?

It seemed his night was not quite over.

The Tree Farm

Corporal Justin Pitts took a knee on the cold, hard ground. Lost in a maze of pine trees deep within Big John's tree farm, Corporal Pitts needed a battle plan. First things first, he had to stop the bleeding. One of those little freaks stabbed him with a candy cane. Why the fuck was that thing so sharp, anyway? Come to think of it, there were a few questions Pitts had in mind. Questions such as *what the fuck are those things?* And *why the fuck were they trying to kill me?*

Corporal Pitts pondered these questions, and more, all while taking in the overpowering aroma of the holiday season. Tree sap and pine needles assaulted his nostrils. He loved the smell, loved the season. This should have been a dream come true. When he responded to a Craigslist advertisement seeking one Marine for a Toys for Tots collection campaign, he never considered the dream might be a nightmare in disguise. A bit more thought on his part would have led him to question why a campaign the Marine Corps took part in yearly was recruiting on Craigslist, but Pitts had never been much of a deep thinker. If he had been, he might have enlisted in a branch of service that taught you more than how to kill, or at least a different job within the Marine Corps. Still, his love of the holiday season, and his good hearted nature may very well have led him here regardless of branch of service.

Pitts unclasped the gold buckle from his white belt, a staple of the Marine Dress Blue uniform, which was widely considered the finest looking United States military dress uniform. A beauty to gaze upon, Dress Blues were a fucking nightmare to wear. Hell, it was a two man job just to button the damn collar on the thing, but Pitts didn't care about that right now, he was simply happy to have the belt. It would serve well as a tourniquet to stop the bleeding from his thigh. He felt a little woozy and was worried about the amount of blood he'd left in the snow.

Pitts had been helping Santa pack up the display when one of the "elves"... mutated or something. Pitts didn't know, and he didn't care either. The *what* was irrelevant. All he knew for sure was that one moment the thing looked human, the next its face was a scarred, burned mess. Razor teeth protruded from its mouth. Fingernails like talons grew in an instant. The creature ran at him, holding a giant, sharpened candy cane—not that it needed the candy cane with the horrific claws it possessed—and screaming like a banshee. Pitts had never heard a sound like that in his life. A guttural, panic inducing sound. Now, they kept screaming at him from somewhere in the trees. They, because with Pitt's luck, of course there would be more than one of those things. Were they toying with him? The pun, unintended as it was, made Pitts laugh. It was laugh or go nuts. Maybe he *already* had gone mad. Because that made more sense than being chased through a tree farm by murderous, mutant elves. It was certainly plausible that he'd lost his marbles. Back in Afghanistan, all of the

Marines had been forced to take Mefloquine once a week to prevent malaria. His squad had lovingly called it malaria Monday. Everyone knew Mefloquine caused crazy ass dreams, but what medical had never told anyone was that in rare cases psychosis had been reported as a side effect. He should have chanced the malaria.

Pitts had to stop himself from going down that rabbit hole. Whether or not he was going mad, all that mattered was getting out of this damn tree farm. If he could do that, he would have plenty of time for a psychological deep dive. Only one man could get him off this fucking farm: Santa.

He had hitched a ride here with Kris Kringle himself, and taking in the scenery from the passenger seat, the size of the farm had impressed Corporal Pitts. He had never seen so many Christmas trees in one place. He hadn't seen a map of the farm, but from what he gathered on the drive in, and the walk to Santa's workshop, Pitts figured he was somewhere in the middle of the farm. He could try to run in one direction, sure. But with the sheer amount of trees on the farm, and known points of reference, it would be easy to get turned around. And who knew what lie on the outer edges of the farm. No, without Santa's guidance, he may never escape the farm.

After Pitts fended off the deranged elf, Santa was nowhere to be found. It was as if he vanished, and in his place, half a dozen of the abominations had appeared. Each one of the creatures equally as deranged and blood-thirsty as his assailant. Wounded, Pitts had taken off like a bat out of hell. He didn't care for his odds of fending off seven knee-high mutants while he was bleeding like a stuck pig.

Pitts removed his dress coat and tossed it in the snow. The jacket restricted far too much, and while he had nothing but a white t-shirt under the jacket, and it was freezing outside, he'd much rather have freedom of movement. He needed to be ready for anything. Pitts rubbed his arms, using the friction to warm himself. If the elves didn't kill him, the cold surely would.

Wanting to test his mobility with the tourniquet, Pitts took a few small steps forward, putting varying amounts of pressure and body weight on the leg to make sure it would hold up. It hurt like a bitch, but it would have to do. His life depended on it.

Hehehehehehehe

Giggling in the trees. Pitts thought it sounded closer than the screeches from earlier. He turned around, peering into the trees for the source of laughter. The falling snow obscured anything further than a few feet in front of him, and the dense rows of pine trees only further blocked his line of sight.

He heard a rustling behind him and turned around in time to see tree branches parting, giving way for a psychotic abomination dressed in classic green and red attire. It rushed straight at Pitts, its tiny legs pistoning, propelling its grotesque body faster than Pitts would have thought possible. Quick as lighting, it closed the distance and swung a severed reindeer antler. Pitts hopped back, narrowly avoiding the antler. A sharp pain shot through his leg. It buckled and he fell flat on his ass, a plume of snow puffing up in the air around him.

Pitts crawled backward as the elf stalked forward. It giggled and stabbed at the air while inching closer to Pitts, a murderous, maniacal expression smeared on its face.

"Don't you think Santa gives us the best toys, Justin?" the elf asked. Its voice pierced Pitts's ears, like nails dragging across a chalkboard.

"What the fuck are you?" asked Pitts.

"I'm an elf, silly! What are you, a dummy?"

Pitts scrambled to his feet. "This is fucking crazy. Why are you doing this?"

"You Marines are naughty boys. And you, Justin, you're on the top of the list. You thought you had gotten away with those things you did. You and your friends did very bad things. *Naughty* things, and Santa said coal wouldn't be enough to fix you." The elf giggled again and leapt through the air.

The elf collided with Pitts hard enough to knock the wind out of him. He fell into the snow once more, tumbling backward, grappling with the elf. That son-of-a-bitch was strong as an ox, and Pitts struggled to gain the upper hand. After some time rolling around in the snow, Pitts managed to mount the elf.

From below, the elf took another swipe at Pitts. This time the antler found its mark. Pitts shirt tore, as did the skin beneath it. A huge gash from pectoral to pectoral appeared, and Pitts wished he had left the jacket on. Any layer of protection would have been better than a plain white T-shirt. Blood splashed across the elf's face, painting its hideous features crimson. It flicked out a long, pointed tongue, running the muscle across its lips and teeth, savoring each drop.

Despite the immense, burning pain from the deep wound, Pitts maintained his position atop the beast. He watched as the monstrosity held its mouth open, trying to catch every drop of blood.

"What a treat, it tastes so sweet!" it rhymed, its gleeful jests made more horrible by its murderous actions.

Cocking his arm, Pitts hit the elf with a haymaker that would have made Mike Tyson proud, but the blow didn't seem to faze the elf; it kicked its legs gleefully and continued to giggle.

"Do it again, you naughty Marine. It's always violence, violence, violence with you naughty jarheads."

Pitts obliged and continued to rain blow after blow upon the elf, shattering its teeth and rearranging its nose. He pounded the elf's face into a bloody pulp, feeling the creature's skeletal structure rearrange from the force of each blow. Pitts didn't relent until his arms were so fatigued he couldn't throw another punch.

When the first punch hadn't so much as phased the elf, Pitts started to worry, but by the time the 21st found its mark, the elf was well and truly fucked.

"Unnggghhh," muttered the elf. It coughed, spraying blood in Pitts' face.

"Just die already, you son-of-a-bitch!" Pitts yelled.

The creature removed the bell from the tip of its hat, and with its last ounce of strength, jingled it. "Santa," it said, "I found that naughty boy. Please don't be mad at me."

The elf lay broken, the snow around it soaked in blood and bits of bone and flesh. The elf's holiday attire was now completely saturated, not only from the snow, but from a massive loss of blood. It had also pissed and shit itself when it expired. Not quite the festive garb it had once been.

Pitts rolled off of the creature and got back to his feet. He had to get out of here, and if what the creature said was the truth, Santa was in on...whatever this was, effectively killing the only plan for survival Pitts had come up with.

Was this some kind of trap to punish him? At least that's what the elf said. Corporal Justin Pitts had a few skeletons in his closet. Many of them gained overseas. How could this *thing* know about any of that?

"Hohoho," a voice bellowed. It was close. "Rudolph, won't you guide my sleigh to that murdering piece of shit?"

"You've gotta be kidding me," said Pitts. He took off, sprinting through the pine trees, not waiting to see what yuletide horrors Santa had in store for him.

Branches whipped Pitts in the face, opening lacerations across his face. Pitts held his hand in front of his face. The last thing he needed was a tree branch impaling an eyeball. He was exhausted, and in great physical pain, bleeding from his chest and the candy cane wound. But he wouldn't stop running, Justin knew that to stop would mean death. Marines weren't taught to retreat, it was kill or be killed, but nothing in the combat training courses mentioned bloodthirsty elves or maniacal holiday heroes. He was in uncharted territory.

Running through the snow would have been difficult on a good day, but with the events of the evening, it was impossible to keep going.

Pitts stopped in his tracks. He leaned forward, chest heaving as he struggled to breathe.

Overhead, bells jingled. Pitts looked in the frosty night sky and couldn't believe what he saw. Just above the trees, eight headless reindeer flying through the sky, their legs moving as if they were running through the air, pulling a giant sleigh behind them.

Santa had arrived with the rest of his demonic helpers.

Justin thought he looked pissed.

He ran deeper into the trees. He wanted no part of that jolly mother fucker. Keeping his eyes on the sleigh, Pitts was distracted and ran into a Christmas tree. His feet left the ground, the momentum propelling him forward until he crashed into the snow beneath him where he held his face and writhed in pain. The collision with the large tree branch broke his nose, and gouts of blood poured out and ran between his fingers. At least his shirt had already been drenched in blood and he needn't worry about ruining it any further.

"Hohoho, that was some funny shit right there, Justin," Santa said. His jovial laugh at odds with the situation at hand.

Santa pulled the reins of the sleigh hard, and to the left. The headless reindeer did a 180 in the sky and took a hard angle toward the ground. The sleigh touched down, and the reindeer halted, kicking a cloud of snow in the air. The reindeer carried with them the stench of the grave. Rotting meat hung from bone, peeling off in strips. Small patches of sporadic tufts of fur all that remained of their once beautiful coats, exposing the gray, rotted flesh underneath.

Santa and the rest of the elves hopped out of the sleigh.

"You put up quite the fight, my dear boy," Santa said. "It's been decades since anyone has killed one of my elves."

Pitts stood up, blood pouring from his nose, and watched Santa walk around the back of the sleigh. When he returned, Pitts noted the giant red sack he brought with him.

"Presents?" he asked Santa.

"Not for you," Santa said, rubbing his belly. Cookie crumbs littered his long, white beard.

"What do you want?"

"Sometimes, Justin, punishing the bad boys can be more gratifying than rewarding the good ones. But you know all about punishing the bad ones, right Corporal Pitts?"

Pitts did, but he wouldn't admit it. "Listen, Santa...or whoever the fuck you are, we did shit, things I'm not proud of. I wish I could take it back, but that's not how it works. War isn't black and white. You sit by and watch people plant bombs in the road. Watch people snipe your friends while they're standing on the road taking a fucking leak and tell me you don't do some fucked up shit to the people responsible. I never did anything to anyone who didn't have it coming. There is no innocent blood on my hands. You don't have to do this."

"The blood on my hand's isn't from the innocent either, Justin. And you are far from innocent, my dear boy," Santa said.

Pitts watched as Santa reached into the sack. He grabbed something with both hands, struggling to pull it free. Slowly, a large, red and white striped pole emerged from the sack. The thing was humongous. No way such a thing could have fit in there. Then again, he was fighting for his life against a killer, magical Santa and his murderous mutant elves, so who the fuck was he to say what could and couldn't happen.

"I checked my list twice, Justin. You're on the wrong one this year," Santa said, grunting as he hefted the rest of the pole from the sack.

The speed at which Santa hoisted the pole over his shoulder and rushed Pitts was shocking. Pitts dove to the left, narrowly avoiding getting flattened by the pole as Santa swung downward as if playing whack a mole. The pole crashed into the ground where Justin stood moments before. Pitts stood up, clutching his chest. It still bled where the elf slashed him, and although the snow softened the blow, it hurt like a motherfucker when he dove to the ground. At least he hadn't been pancaked by the North Pole that Santa was toting around.

Pitts looked around. A horrible situation had become even more dire. The elves had formed a circle around the two men. They held giant candy canes with pointed tips. In unison, they stabbed them into the ground, lifted them up and repeated. Again and Again they stabbed the ground with their candy canes. Pitts was in the fight of his life, and to the Christmas crew, this was nothing more than a schoolyard fight.

Something hard smashed into Pitt's rib cage and knocked him sideways. The elves had distracted him, and Santa took advantage of his lapse in focus. Justin thought a few of his ribs might be broken. He was on all fours now, trying to gather himself as the cold snow stung his hands and knees. He looked up as Santa walked toward him, dragging the pole behind him.

Thump. Thump. Thump. Pitts heard the candy cane closest to him smash into the ground. The elf wielding it so close that with each strike at the ground fresh powder sprayed Pitts in the face.

"Are you ready, Justin?" Santa asked.

Pitts looked at the candy cane once more before locking eyes with Santa. "Fuck you," he spat.

Santa lifted the pole over his head once more.

With all the speed he could muster, Pitts kicked his leg at the elf nearest him. The elf doubled over and dropped the candy cane to the ground. Justin snatched the candy cane and thrusted the tip upward, driving it through Santa's lower jaw. Santa dropped the pole behind him. His lifeless knees hit the ground as his head, now skewered on the candy cane, slid further down it. Bits of skull and brain stuck to the candy cane as blood gushed from Santa's head. The large candy cane took up too much space in Santa's skull, and one of his eyeballs popped out of the socket, dangling from it by nothing more than optical nerves. Blood and brain tissue stained the snow around Santa. Kris Kringle had eaten his last cookie.

Pitts stood up and looked around at the elves. They no longer pounded the ground with their candy canes. They stood, mouths agape, silent in defeat.

Justin shivered. He had survived Santa, but what did that matter if he was going to freeze to death, anyway?

He walked over to Santa and stripped him down. The red velvet costume with its white fleece interior looked especially inviting, even with the discarded bits of brain stuck to the material. If the suit kept Santa warm, it would do the same for him. He threw the pants on over his own and slipped into the jacket. After he buttoned it, he brushed flecks of skull off his shoulder. They fell to the ground, macabre snowflakes, each one its own unique shape. He left the hat on Santa's ruined head. The candy cane pierced through it, and it would be too difficult to remove that hat.

Pitts grabbed Santa's magic sack and tossed it behind the driver seat of the sleight. He stood there for a moment before hopping in and grabbing the reins, looking over to the elves. "You guys coming or what?" he asked.

The elves picked their canes up off of the ground and piled into the back of the sleigh.

Pitts snapped the reins, and the reindeer took flight.

"Merry Christmas to all," Pitts said.

"And to all a good night!" the elves replied.

Stasis

Lynne opened her eyes and shuddered. She sat up and kicked her legs over the side of the stasis pod, arching her back to get the kinks out. After a long sleep, the first stretch always sounded like microwave popcorn. She crossed her arms, rubbing her hands along them in a pitiful attempt to warm up. A plume of breath escaped her lips.

"Fuck, it's cold. What's wrong with the heat?"

Lynne waggled her feet underneath her pod, searching blindly for her slippers. She gave up her search and walked around the edge of the pod to the datapad at the foot of it.

No readings out of the ordinary. Why am I awake?

Lynne looked around. As the fog of sleep rolled off of her, her situational awareness strengthened. As she realized the bay lights were off a siren kicked on, its shrill cry piercing the darkness. The emergency lighting system kicked on shortly after.

What the fuck is going on? Where is everybody?

All five of the other pods were open, all of them empty.

Lynne walked over to the maintenance terminal and navigated through the readouts.

Twenty-five years, she thought to herself. *We're supposed to be asleep for another five. Who aborted stasis?*

The mining expedition had been a success. There were one hundred crews that had deployed to various moons throughout the Andromeda galaxy. The mission was as simple as they come: mine the moons. Harvest any and all precious metals, load as much as possible into the ship, and get out. Upon completion of the mission, crew members re-entered cryo-sleep where they remained until their rendezvous with the parent ship, the New Dawn.

Lynne continued to parse through maintenance logs, searching for clues. Being well informed could mean the difference between life and death on one of these missions. If there were an issue with the ship it only made sense to know about it before walking around in the dark.

According to the readout, a status abnormality had caused another crewmember, Mike, to prematurely exit stais. His internal body temperature had steadily risen, triggering the process. After Mike's pod started the emergency medical reawakening protocol, someone had opened the other pods manually.

Why would Mike do something like that?

Protocol dictated that only Decker, their medical specialist, was to be released in the event of a medical emergency.

Lynne reached the end of the data logs. There was no mention of any emergency aside from Mike's temperature. The ship's AI didn't function under emergency power, so she would need to make her way to the command center to gather more information.

I've gotta find the others, maybe they know what's going on. But why didn't anyone stick around to fill me in?

Lynne walked over to her locker. She grabbed a t-shirt, sweatpants, and a pair of sneakers. Fully clothed, she exited the stasis room. The lighting situation in the main hall was no better.

Lynne looked around, gathering her bearings. It had been years since she'd last been awake and she still felt off from the shortened awakening process. You never realize how necessary an acclimation period is after stasis until you don't get one.

Walking through the corridor, Lynne decided to swing by the sickbay before heading to the command center. With Mike's readouts being what they were, there was a high probability that both he and Decker were in the sickbay. They may have answers. The rest of the crew could be anywhere.

Using one hand to run alongside the wall as guidance, Lynne continued down the corridor, her other hand shielding her eyes from the emergency lights. The person who designed them couldn't have been too bright. It made no sense for emergency lighting to strobe in that manner. First off, it could cause a fucking seizure. Second, every time the light kicked on and off, it decimated your night vision. Lynne thought that was proof in the pudding the assholes designing the transports had never actually set foot in one, never mind spent an extended amount of time living on one.

Her sneaker struck the deck and squealed as it slipped out from underneath her, sending her crashing to the floor.

Her body and clothes were wet with whatever she had slipped on. The floor was saturated with God knows what.

She wiped her hands on her pants and took a deep breath. A harsh stink assaulted her nose, a smell so strong it was no small wonder that she hadn't picked it out sooner. She could almost taste the metallic tang. In between the pulsing lights, Lynne saw blood smeared across her pant legs.

"What the fuck?" she screamed, rolling onto her hands and knees.

The viscera-covered deck made it difficult to regain her balance. As she pushed herself up something collapsed under the weight of her palm and she heard a sickening squelch. A nasty, wet tearing. Something sharp scraped along her arm as it sunk into whatever the fuck it was. The lighting above flashed, revealing the disgusting sight. The decimated corpse of a crewmember on the ground. Her hand had pressed into the cadavers' torn open chest cavity. The body's shattered rib cage had cut her as her hand slid deeper into the wound. If you could even call something that catastrophic a wound.

Lynne turned her head. Her stomach turned over, but she could only dry heave, her stomach empty of food. The small amount of stomach acid that came up left a vile, rancid taste in her mouth.

A mass of small, black, worm-like creatures—each one maybe three or four inches in length—filled the open cavity. Lynne had never seen larvae like these before. They certainly weren't maggots. The creatures writhed over one another, eager to feast on the corpse. The deceased crew member's internal organs were strewn about the hall, leaving spatterings of gore along the walls and ceiling. Blood dripped from the ceiling, landing in Lynne's hair. She gagged. The sight and smell were horrendous. Far too much for her to handle. She needed to get the fuck out of here before whatever left behind such a mess discovered her.

At last Lynne stood up, but she almost slipped again. This time she kept her footing and raced down the hall, listening for sounds of life within the otherwise deserted halls. The combined noise of her heart jackhammering in her chest and her feet slapping the floor as she ran made it difficult to listen to her surroundings.

She ran as fast as her legs would take her until the surge of adrenaline subsided. Now out of breath, she crept onward toward the sickbay, keeping her hand against the cool, metal wall for guidance. It wouldn't do to get turned around in the dark. Not when *something* had so easily eviscerated her crewmate. She thought again of the exposed cavity. The decimated bones and exposed internal organs.

Lynne didn't know which one of her friends had been murdered; the remains of the corpse so utterly wrecked it was unidentifiable. She recalled the body, thinking that maybe it had been a female member of the crew, Kat or Stacy, but with the damage done there was no way she could be sure.

She stopped in her tracks, a sealed door blocking her progress.

The sickbay.

Lynne stabbed her finger at the screen, punching her code on the panel. An error message flashed across it. *Shit. Slow down. Slow is smooth.* She took a deep breath, calming her nerves before attempting her code a second time. The panel turned green. A cheerful ping sounded, which did little to make her feel better. Sure, she got out of the dark hallway and further away from the dead body, but she had no idea where the thing responsible for the corpse was hiding. It was bad enough she'd already made plenty of noise, no need to continue announcing her presence.

She gulped, trying to swallow the lump in her throat as she entered the sickbay, following the wall along the right side of the room and using her feet to probe the darkness in between flashes of emergency lighting. She knew there should be an emergency supply chest somewhere along the wall; all of the essential areas of the ship had them. The trouble was finding it in the dark and not breaking her neck tripping over it.

Lynne stumbled over something. The locker. At least she didn't snap her neck like she feared she might, although, given the circumstances, maybe that would have been a blessing in disguise.

She dropped to her knees, opened the latch, and flipped the lid. She rummaged through the locker before at last finding what she was searching for—a headlamp. At least now she wouldn't be at the mercy of the ship's bullshit emergency lighting system. After pulling the straps tight and raising its red-plastic tint, Lynne was ready to continue now that she could see short distances in front of her.

She swirled her head right to left, taking in her surroundings. The entire room was a mess. Viscera painted the room a grisly mosaic of blood and entrails. Goose pimples dotted her flesh, whether from the cold or the horror, she couldn't say. Likely a combination of the two.

In the middle of the room sat a gurney. The sheets were strewn about, stained with something, but she couldn't tell what because of the eerie red glow from her headlamp. One thing was certain, someone had been in here.

She moved closer and could see more of the black worms from earlier, wriggling around on the sheets. A baseball-sized mass of them crawled over and around each other. Another smaller cluster of them detached from the mass and landed on the floor with a wet, slapping noise. The impact sent them flying in every direction, some of them narrowly missing Lynne. The sight of them brought back further memories of the corpse, and for the second time, her stomach turned on end, leaving her feeling queasy.

"Lynne…" a voice croaked from behind the gurney.

It was Decker.

He sat slumped against the metal wall of the sickbay, a large pool of blood beneath him, the scarlet substance continuing to grow around him. Worms wriggled all over his body. They were everywhere. The hair on his head swayed about as if blown by the wind as the creatures moved along his scalp. His mouth hung slack. They crawled from the opening, plopping to the ground with a wet smack. He didn't seem to notice.

Or maybe he no longer cared. Lynne couldn't say.

"What the fuck is going on, Decker?"

"It's Mike," he said, his voice a harsh, raspy thing. "He…woke me up… He was sick, had a fever. I helped him to the sickbay. As soon as I got him on the table he started puking up these worms. Everywhere. Hundreds of the things."

"Jesus Christ…"

"He died. Not long after he puked those things up. Right there on that table. I saw it with my own two eyes. But he's not dead. He came back…"

"What the fuck do you mean he came back?"

"I mean he was dead, and then he wasn't. After I was sure there was nothing more I could do for him, I rinsed myself off in the sink, those things had been all over me, and I was covered in vomit and blood. I heard something moving behind me, at first just the sheet rustling. I thought maybe it was just from his body twitching post mortem, but then there was this awful noise, almost like something tearing… I turned around and he was sitting up, screaming bloody murder. But it was like no scream I'd ever heard before. It wasn't like he was in pain; it was something primal. There were…things coming out of his back. Some kind of appendages…four of them. They looked like spider legs. The ends of them were razor-sharp."

"You're telling me that Mike died, came back to life, and grew a set of spider legs? Decker, you've lost a lot of blood; you're hallucinating. We need to get you patched up and then we can figure out what's going on."

"C'mon, you don't believe that," he said. "You've seen something. I can see it in your face. Why else would you be skulking around in the dark, shaking like a leaf? You're terrified."

Lynne crossed the sickbay and stopped at the sink. There was a plasma torch on the counter. She picked it up. "You're right. I found a dead body. I couldn't tell if it was Kat or Stacy—the body was too fucked up—but what you're telling me is absurd. It doesn't make sense." She walked back to Decker. "And where the fuck is Mike? Why isn't he here?"

"He's not Mike anymore. I told you, he's dead. Whatever that thing is, it isn't Mike. It attacked me. Sliced me open with ease and then puked up a bunch of those fucking things. Got those fucking worms all over me. I tried to fry it with that torch, but it skittered off. I don't know where it is now."

"Shit." Lynne paced back and forth. "Then who woke the rest of us up?"

"It had to have been that thing. After he took off, I passed out. It wasn't me."

"So, Mike is some kind of monster, but he's still able to work the transport's controls? Are you telling me he can still think?"

"I guess so. How the fuck should I know? I'm telling

you what I saw. You need to get out of here. Get to the command deck, signal the New Dawn and request an emergency evacuation. Once you've done that, make your way back to the stasis room. Once inside, use this torch to seal the hatch before you enter one of the pods. Hopefully, that will be enough to keep Mike out."

"What about you?"

"What about me? I'm bleeding out and I can feel something inside of me. I think it's those worms. I'm burning up and I think whatever happened to Mike is happening to me. From here on out, you need to assume that I am like him. Do not trust me."

Lynne ran her hands through her hair, letting out a sigh. This was too much. It had to be some kind of nightmare. Some sort of error with the sleep systems in the pods.

"Fuck. I'm sorry, Decker. I'll figure this out." She turned and exited the infirmary. With a clear objective, maybe she'd be able to focus long enough to not succumb to a panic attack.

Her sense of time was in disarray. Minutes of skulking through the shadows felt like hours. The constant rush of chemicals from her body's fight or flight response took a toll on her. Her entire body throbbed, aching as if she had awakened from a horrible vehicle accident, not from cryo-sleep. As she approached the area where she had discovered her disemboweled crewmate, she steeled her nerves in anticipation of seeing her friend's eviscerated remains a second time.

The body was gone. Vanished into thin air. If not for the gore and worms plastered everywhere in the area, Lynne would have thought she had simply imagined the entire scenario.

Click-click-click.

A sound like animal claws against the metal floor. It was coming from the ventilation shaft running along the base of the wall.

Click-Click-Click. Closer.

Lynne aimed her headlamp at the vent but the dim red glow did little to cut through the darkness in the shaft.

Stepping back, she barely registered a flash of movement behind the vent cover before something smashed into it, sending it flying across the corridor.

Two long, barbed, segmented legs appeared from the shaft, grasping for purchase on either side of the opening. The creature used those horrific legs to pull itself out. Its head emerged, what was left of the victim's human flesh dripping off of its skull like wax dripping down the side of a candle. Black, soulless eyes sunk into hollowed orbital cavities. Its jaw dangled from tattered strands of flesh, dragging uselessly across the floor as the creature pushed its way out of the vent.

"Jesus Christ, what the fuck is that?" Lynne said.

She pointed the plasma torch at the nightmare creature, squeezing the trigger mechanism. Lynne held her weapon steady as the creature shrieked, writhing in pain. The torch's super-hot plasma burned through one of the appendages, slicing it clean off. The abomination whipped its head back and forth, waving its other leg wildly around while the stump of the first smoldered.

Lynne pointed the torch at the creature again, ready to take its other leg off. Once more, she squeezed the trigger, coughing violently as the acrid smoke drifted into her nostrils and the smell of charred meat filled the hallway.

The creature, now lying helplessly on the floor, stared at Lynne.

Didn't Decker say Mike had four of those legs? Does that mean there are more of those…things?

Lynne inspected the monstrosity closer, unless Decker was mistaken, it couldn't be Mike. Whoever it was had mutated into some kind of monster, similar to what happened to Mike, but anatomically different.

It tried to bite Lynne as she got closer, but the strands of gristle holding the jaw in place snapped, leaving it defanged *and* declawed. Lynne screamed, a primal howl from the depths of her soul. She stomped on the creature's skull repeatedly, until there was nothing left but a pulpy mess of bone fragments, blood, and brain matter. And worms.

Lynne turned and sprinted through the hallway, running as fast as her legs would take her. She was no longer concerned with moving silently. She needed to get to the control room and send a distress signal. She knew any thoughts of rescue had been foolish, who could possibly arrive before her untimely demise? Still, she had to let the New Dawn know that something was horribly wrong. She did not know where the rest of the crew was, including Mike. She had to assume that if this corpse and Mike had both somehow turned into monsters, the rest of the crew might have as well.

What did Decker say? He could feel something inside of him? Shit.

Lynne made her way along the corridor, slowing as she approached the command room. Hunched over, she placed her hands on her knees, trying to control her breathing. After a few moments had passed, she punched her password into the panel next to the door.

The command entrance slid open.

Lynne held the torch in front of her as she snuck inside. Against all odds, she had arrived at her destination but there was more work to be done and she couldn't afford carelessness in the home stretch.

She approached the communication terminal and trained her headlamp on it, once again punching in her pin. No dice.

"Shit!"

With the ship being on emergency power, two-way communication was no longer a possibility. She would have to send a distress signal and hope that whoever received the transmission, whether that be the New Dawn or some other ship in the vicinity, received the communication and would proceed with caution. She cursed herself for forgetting such an important bit of information, but given the circumstances, who could blame her?

But what about the creatures? Lynne could only assume anyone missing had been transformed, and with no way to communicate, any responding ship would be woefully unprepared for the horrors inside the vessel.

Lynne saw only one option. She had to prepare a self-destruct sequence. If she could somehow seal the creatures off from the rest of the ship, and manage to get herself to a capsule, she could blow the ship without killing herself in the process. That was a big if.

Even if she didn't send out the distress signal, the New Dawn was still scheduled to rendezvous in five years for pickup. She might not make it that long, but there was no way to know if those things could survive if left alone.

Self-destruction really was her only option to ensure the creatures would kill no more.

Plop.

Something landed on her head. She swatted her hair, brushing something onto the floor. It was a worm.

"Fuck," she whispered, taking a step back and looking at the ceiling.

Another creature clung to the ceiling. This one with

four legs, exactly as Decker had described the thing that had once been Mike.

The Mike creature dropped from the ceiling, its newly grown appendages taking the impact and supporting the husk of Mike, suspending its body in the air. The creature reminded her of a villain in one of those comic book movies people on Earth used to watch, long before the planet was destroyed. It let loose an ear-splitting shriek and lashed out at Lynne with one of the legs. She tried to jump back but wasn't quick enough. The razor-sharp edge of the leg cut through her shirt, slicing the skin just above her navel. She fell flat on her ass and dropped the plasma torch.

Mike's reanimated corpse stalked toward her in herky-jerky motions, its jaws clicking, worms falling from its mouth instead of saliva.

Lynne scurried backward, using her hands and heels to scoot back as fast as she could until she bumped into the terminal.

The thing continued forward, seemingly unconcerned with its prey.

Lynne ran her hand along the deck, searching for the discarded torch. She brushed against something on the deck.

Got it!

Pointing the torch at the creature, it was close enough that aim wasn't necessary. A fiery burst seared the necrotic flesh of the thing that was once Mike. It shrieked. Maybe it had been unconcerned a moment ago, but Lynne was about to put the fear of God in the abomination.

Lynne kept the torch trained on him, burning flesh. It sizzled and popped. Strips of bubbling skin fell to the floor. The smell was horrendous, but Lynne didn't let up until Mike crumpled to the ground.

The moment she let up on the trigger, the creature resumed its hunt. The tenacity of the thing was undeniable. Lynne squeezed the trigger once more.

The flame sputtered and died. *Out of fuel. I'm fucked.*

It stopped in front of Lynne. Its face a charred mess and body still engulfed in flames. The horror summoned the last of its strength, pushing up from the floor with those horrific legs until it towered over Lynne's cowering form. Its mouth opened, stretching impossibly wide as a wave of worms shot out from its mouth, splattering Lynne with their filth. As the stream of maggot-infused vomit cut off, the creature collapsed to the ground. Mike was dead.

Again.

She spit, flinging worms from her mouth. They crawled over her body, wriggling about, finding their way into her wounds. Any hole or opening was a point of entry for the vile larvae. The worms ate their way through her flesh. The teeth, though small, easily tore through skin and muscle. They attached themselves to her spine, taking over her central nervous system. Some of them made their way through her skull, latching onto her brain.

Lynne could…feel them. The worms were an invasive parasite. They devoured the host and manipulated its body to spread more parasites, using the host's own mind as a tool. Helpless to resist, the host—Lynne—became a prisoner in her own body.

Powerless, Lynne was forced to watch as the worms guided her body back to the communication terminal, effortlessly parsing through her memories, they found the necessary codes and activated the distress signal. They marched her back to the stasis room where they input her pin on the datapad.

The pod opened.

Lynne removed her clothes, entered the pod, and lay down. The lid closed, locking in place with an audible click.

While Lynne hibernated, the parasites would wait.

The Hale Koa Incident

The sun shone overhead, beating down on Danny Robinson's bare back as he unloaded a cooler full of Corona Light from the bed of his Chevy Colorado. He hadn't bothered to put sunscreen on, and his back had already reddened. Dan wasn't worried about the long term effects of the sun on his skin. For the last eight months of training, the senior Marines in his platoon had made it clear to him he probably wasn't coming home from Iraq alive, and so Danny had stopped caring about things that could have long-term health repercussions. When faced with the genuine possibility of being blown to smithereens, many of life's other hazards seemed, at worst, trivial. Even still, it dawned on him while unloading the cooler that while he might not give a rat's ass about long-term sun exposure effects, he'd rather not get sun-poisoning, or massive blisters all over his back. Oh well, too late for that today, but that was something to think about next time. He was stationed on Marine Corps Base Hawaii, in Kaneohe Bay, a literal tropical paradise. There would be plenty of time to learn from one bad sunburn.

Danny's best friend, Randy, opened the passenger door and hopped out of the truck. He approached Danny and slapped his sun-burnt back. "Here, let me help you with that kayak, bro."

Danny winced, his back going ram-rod straight, pulling his shoulders back from the pain like he was trying to smash a grapefruit in between his shoulder blades. "Yeah, thanks. It's too bad Ashley couldn't get on base. I know you were excited to get her out here on the water with you."

Randy spit a chaw-stained, brown stream in the sand. "Yep, but that's the green weenie for you. Uncle Sam fucks you anyway it can."

"Speaking of the green weenie… shit has been weird around here, so if we're going to get on the water, we need to get there quickly. The Military Police have been out in force lately, and you know how those dickheads love to bust fellow Marines any chance they can. Typical POG fucks, anything to shaft a grunt. And the new base commander won't hesitate to fry our asses if he finds out we took off while the entire base is on restriction," Danny said.

Randy laughed. "You're right about that. Those pricks are mad because when they go home to their girlfriends they fantasize about infantryman, not knowing that their boyfriends were too pussy to actually fight when they enlisted."

The two Marines lifted the kayak off the rack Danny had mounted to his truck, placing it on the sand beside them. Danny locked the doors to the truck and hid the key in a magnetic holder inside of the wheel well. The last thing he wanted was to lose the keys in the ocean. He would be in a world of shit if he had to call base police to tow the truck, especially when the beach was off limits.

Neither of the men knew what to make of the restrictions. They extended far beyond anything either of them had experienced before. A complete lockdown of MCBH. Nobody was allowed to enter or exit the base, a rule that applied to both military and civilian personnel. The restriction had come down in the dead of night, and whatever the reason for the lockdown, they weren't kidding about it being airtight. Many of the officer staff lived in houses or apartments off base, and the MPs wouldn't even let them on base.

That was a week ago, and nothing had changed since.

The highest-ranking Marine in his platoon who had been on base when the lockdown struck was Sergeant Gallo, and even he had only been around because he lived in the barracks, a rarity for someone of his rank. Everything was being kept hush, and if anyone knew what was going on, they were keeping quiet about it. Randy had told him that in his seven years in the Marine Corps—five of them stationed at Kaneohe Bay—he couldn't recall a single time an entire base had been restricted, much less the use of its beaches revoked.

Danny grabbed a Corona and bit the cap off with his teeth. "So, have you talked to Ashley? What does she have to say about this?"

Randy winced at Danny's blatant disregard for his oral health. "She says she understands, but she's pretty fucking pissed about it. You know how she gets. She claims the Marine Corps is up to no good, destroying the environment. Conducting crimes against humanity. You know, the usual shit. I don't know, man, it's a lot. It really sucks when the woman you're dating is vehemently against the organization you're a part of."

Randy took a sip from his beer and continued venting. "Hell, man, you remember she flew out to Hilo to protest us training at Pohakuloa. I'm still catching shit for that, from Marines *and* from her."

Danny laughed. "Yeah, that was fucked up. I kind of get her point though. She lives here. If I was a local and there was just an influx of military dudes moving here every year, a revolving door of Type-A assholes treating the island like a dump and acting like a bunch of drunken pricks all the time, I'd be pissed, too. And that's before you even bring the destruction and pollution of the environment into the conversation."

"Don't be a pussy, bro."

"I'm not being a pussy. I'm just saying I get where your girl is coming from. She's got a solid point, when she isn't spouting conspiracy theory bullshit about the military."

"Man, shut up and let's get this kayak in the water."

The two Marines hefted the kayak up and made their way across the sand. It was hot, and burned their feet. Danny loved the feel of the grains on his feet. The way they tickled the skin in between his toes.

Small, frothy waves broke against the shore, wetting his ankles. Danny breathed in the ocean's scent. He'd grown up in Rhode Island, the Ocean State, but the Atlantic Ocean was an absolute dump compared to the Pacific Ocean, and that was a hill he would die on. All manner of waste littered the beaches back home, from empty beer bottles, food containers, even drug paraphernalia. One thing was for certain: Danny couldn't remember seeing discarded heroin needles at any of the beaches on Oahu, something he had seen on more than one occasion back home.

They placed the kayak in the pristine water, hopped in, and made their way out into the ocean. They planned on paddling out far beyond where they could touch the bottom. There was something exhilarating about swimming in open water without a safety net like the ocean floor. It was a beautiful day, and as always, the water was crystal clear. Another far cry from the Atlantic. You could get a good way from land and still see the ocean floor around here. You had to be ready for something like that, because if you weren't you might just find your ass drowned in the ocean.

As they were paddling, Danny's mind drifted off. The thought of leaving this tropical paradise he now thought of as home, only to live in a desert where he was convinced he would meet a violent, untimely demise depressed the shit out of him.

"Asshole, you gonna paddle or what?" Randy interrupted Danny's daydream.

"Yeah, yeah." He paddled, quickly getting in sync with Randy. "I was just thinking about the ocean. I love it out here. Never was much of a beach guy before getting stationed here. It isn't this clean back home. Certainly not this beautiful."

"I'll bet the water in Rhode Island is better than anything we've got back home."

"Anything beats the hell out of Vidor, Texas," Danny laughed.

"Keep talking shit and I'll drown you out here, city boy."

Danny punched Randy in the shoulder and laughed again. "Man, stop pretending you can swim. I know all you have is little shitwater creeks back home."

"Yeah, hilarious. Let's get further out and see who can't swim."

The men continued their voyage, and despite the pristine, clear water, they could no longer see the bottom.

Danny wasn't sure how deep they were, but they were far enough away that despite his excellent swimming ability, he wouldn't want to attempt a swim back without the kayak. And although Randy claimed to be an excellent swimmer, Danny wasn't so sure about that. Despite the bravado, he seemed a bit timid out here, surrounded by the Pacific Ocean and its seemingly endless biodiversity. Danny didn't blame him. They were trained killers, neither of them wanted to admit they were scared to be this far out in the ocean.

Almost as if Randy sensed what Danny was thinking and had to prove himself, he stopped paddling. "You want to hop in and do some snorkeling?"

Danny grabbed his snorkel. "Are you sure you want to? The last time we went swimming you weren't allowed to hang out for like a week, like you're Ashley's little bitch. She went ballistic on you." Shaking his head and laughing, Danny continued, "I can't believe she actually thinks that the Marine Corps is conducting experiments on sea life out here. First off, there's not a Marine on the planet smart enough to conduct any kind of experiment not written in crayon."

Randy's face went red and he bit his lip. "The crayons wouldn't make it past snack time, never mind any experiments. But yeah, in all seriousness, I get what you're saying. It's fucking embarrassing, but sometimes I have to let her think she's in charge if I want to get laid. I don't know where she gets the idea about experimenting on sea life from. She goes off on these rants that don't make any sense, and she's got *zero* evidence to support her theories. She claims they've done something to the ocean, and that's why you don't see many rays or squid around Kaneohe Bay anymore. I asked her how big the stick up her ass was. Needless to say, I haven't gotten laid in a while. Sometimes

I don't even know why we're together if she hates Marines so much."

"Well, you could always take a video of all the fish out here, show her there's nothing to worry about. Nothing wrong with the sea life as far as I can tell from this kayak. I bet she's got the fucking tin foil hat on right now, thinking about all the reasons why we could be locked down.

"Yeah, you're right. Maybe I'll show her the ocean life here and tell her the only thing more beautiful is her. It's just corny enough that it might work. Maybe her blood pressure will go down a bit and she can calm down, find something else to stress about." Randy took his phone from his pocket, complete with a case that allowed the phone to go as deep as fifty feet and remain waterproof.

Danny polished off the last of his beer and tossed it in the ocean. When he realized what he had done, he tried to snatch the bottle, but it had already sunk beyond his reach.

"Are you fucking kidding me?" Randy said. "You really just chucked that bottle in the ocean after talking about how beautiful this place was compared to Rhode Island. You're a fucking scumbag dude. I don't want to hear your bullshit about Texas again."

Randy attached a handle and a lanyard to the phone case, and Danny couldn't help but think what a good idea that was, attaching it to his phone so he wouldn't lose it in the ocean. Maybe the genepool in Vidor wasn't quite as shallow as he thought. He'd never admit that to Randy, though. He loved to bust the man's balls.

"Let's do this, bro. Time to enjoy this paradise, because for all we know, our future might be nothing but blood in the sand." Randy stood up, bit down on the snorkel mouthpiece, and jumped into the beautiful, crystal clear ocean. Not one to miss out on any action, Danny followed suit.

He swam below the surface briefly before emerging and blowing water from his snorkel. Danny couldn't ask for a better cap to the weekend. The water was perfect, and although the day was hotter than usual, the temperature of the ocean water was perfect, providing an excellent respite from the sun.

Randy broke the surface soon after Danny. "Man, I'm glad we came out here. I hope we don't get caught, though. We are *fucked* if anyone finds us out here. I can't afford to get busted down in rank again."

"Okay, so don't get caught." Danny dove below the surface once more and Randy joined him. The two men swam through the ocean together, taking in the beauty of one of nature's true marvels. Despite the relative cleanliness of the ocean, a small Styrofoam coffee cup floated by, and Danny couldn't help but feel sad. What might this ocean look like if humanity were a better tenant? Hopefully Earth wouldn't purge itself of humans before people finally pulled their heads out of their asses and started talking about climate change and ocean conservation in a serious, non-political manner. Sure, the military did its fair share of destroying the earth, but as an individual, Danny did his best to be eco-friendly. He loved nature, and days like today hammered that home. The thought pissed him off, and then he remembered that a few minutes ago he had been the asshole tossing trash in the ocean. Maybe he wasn't really a caring steward of nature's wonders. Maybe it was just something he told himself, knowing damn well he was just as bad as anyone else in that regard.

Despite the beautiful weather and clarity of the ocean surrounding him, the waters lacked the usual… life one would typically find around here. There were smaller fish, yes, but where were the sharks, the rays, and the squid?

Danny couldn't recall seeing a single one, an oddity in these waters for sure.

Danny looked at Randy and signaled to his friend that he intended to surface. Randy followed him up. "We should get back to the kayak," Danny said. "I want to head back to shore."

"What, already? Why?"

"Something's up. I have a weird feeling, I don't know, like something is wrong."

"Jesus, maybe I should break up with Ashley; you can swoop in and be her rebound. The two of you would get along great."

Despite Randy clearly not wanting to go back, Danny was relieved when he swam alongside him back to the kayak. They reached the craft and Danny climbed over the edge, ready to head back to shore. Randy tread water next to the kayak, spitting a fountain of sea water in the air like the giant man-child he was.

Danny had hoped that getting out of the water would ease the suffocating dread he had felt in the open ocean, but it had done nothing to ease his nerves. If anything, he felt as if he were in imminent danger, even though in the boat he was not quite the sitting duck he had been in the ocean.

There was something wrong, he was sure of it. An indefinable quality. The air was still. The water, unusually calm. Despite the warm weather, Danny shivered.

Randy floated in the water, arms crossed over the side of the kayak. "I'm going to stay here for a bit. I'm not ready to go back yet. The water is nice."

"C'mon man, let's just get out of here. I really don't like the vibes I'm getting right now," Danny said.

"The vibes you're getting? I think I'm okay, Miss Cleo. I know you think us cowboys can't swim, but I assure you,

I'm good." Randy laughed, showing a blatant dismissal of Danny's unease, further pissing Danny off.

Regardless, there was nothing to be done but wait for Randy to stop acting like a douche. He couldn't force Randy back on the kayak. The best he could hope for was for Randy to hurry up and decide he'd rather drink a beer than float around aimlessly. That gave him an idea. Danny reached under his seat and grabbed a beer. "You want another one?"

"Sure, might as well."

Danny grabbed a cold one for Randy and popped the top with his teeth again, before passing the beer to his friend. "You're really just going to float there? Something is up, man. I don't know *what*, but something is off. I can feel it."

"Relax, man. I'm going to hang out right here, enjoy my beer, and then we can head back to shore. It's not like I want to be out here all day, anyway. Besides, I'm almost finished with *Ghost of Tsushima*, and the Iki Island Expansion just came out. I want to try to beat it before the new *Aliens* game comes out on Tuesday."

"Oh yeah, I forgot about those games. I really haven't touched my PlayStation much in the last few months. I'll play *Aliens* with you when that comes out. Shit, I'll preorder it as soon as you get your ass back in this kayak and we get back to the barracks."

"Sounds like a plan to… shit, what the fuck was that?" Randy screamed, but his head quickly dipped under water, killing the shout after a brief moment. After a few moments, his head reappeared.

"Dude, what the fuck was that? Get in the boat!"

"Something bit me. I don't know, I'm bleeding!"

A pool of red-tinged ocean water spread around

Randy, who was now flailing his arms and legs, clearly in the midst of a panic attack.

Danny reached out and grabbed Randy underneath both of his arms, pulling, while Randy pushed himself up and out of the water into the kayak. Randy held his hands over his left calf.

"Let me see it," said Danny.

"Shit man, it hurts." Randy let go of his leg.

Danny grimaced. It was bad. A large, wide gash ran vertically along the muscle. Blood poured out of the wound, and Danny was pretty sure he could see the bone, but with the blood coming out so fast it was hard to tell for sure.

Danny looked around the kayak. "I've got to stop this bleeding," he said. Countless hours of combat survival and combat lifesaver courses ran through his mind. He reached for the backpack underneath his seat, rummaging through the bag's contents. "Fuck, there has got to be *something here.*"

A pocket knife.

"Okay, that'll work," Danny said to himself. He took a T-shirt from Randy's bag and tore a strip from it. Muscle memory set in, and Danny tied the strip around Randy's leg above the wound but below the kneecap. He grabbed the pocketknife, closed the blade, and inserted it into the strip of cloth. Using it as a windlass, he twisted the pocketknife over and over, until finally the blood flow slowed to a trickle.

"Okay, hold on, I've almost got this," Danny told his injured friend. He bit his lip. He had to think of something he could use as a securing mechanism for the windlass, otherwise it would just come loose if either he or Randy could not hold it in place.

He rummaged around in the backpack some more. His eyes fell on the soda bottle Randy had used for his rum and

Coke concoction. "Bingo." Danny uncapped the bottle and began peeling at the red plastic underneath the lip. He worked meticulously, taking care not to break the plastic. It was the one thing they had that could work. If he fucked it up, or broke the plastic, Randy was a dead man.

The red plastic ring slid off the mouth of the bottle. "Got it!" Danny shouted. He slipped the ring over the pocket knife as much as he could force it without breaking the plastic. It would have to hold. There was no other way. With the securing plastic ring over the knife, Danny took one last strip of the t-shirt he had torn up and tied one end around the plastic, and the other end around Randy's leg. He hoped it would hold. "Listen, Randy. I don't know how long this plastic is going to hold. You need to monitor it. If it snaps, you're going to have to hold that knife as tight as you can to keep that tourniquet on. I'm going to row, but if you can help, I need you to. Are you up to it?"

"Yeah, I think so. I feel a little woozy, but I think I can help."

"Don't overdo it. Let's work on getting back. We can take a break if you're feeling sick. With the tourniquet on we have enough time to paddle back and get you to the hospital."

Randy moaned, and Danny thought he might be worse off than he was letting on. Maybe the *esprit de corps* the Marine Corps drills into you from the moment your feet hit the yellow footprints kept his friend pushing, even though he probably felt like he was dying.

The two men paddled. Danny kept a slow, deliberate pace, hoping Randy could handle it without dropping out. This was a bad idea. Why didn't Randy listen to him? He'd told him there was something wrong, and now Randy's carefree nature had come up to bite him. Literally.

Danny leaned forward to check on Randy's tourniquet,

but something hit the side of the kayak. A thunderous crack sounded, like wood splitting, and for a moment Danny thought he would go flying over the edge of the kayak.

Not good, Danny thought. Whatever had attacked Randy wasn't finished with them yet. Danny surveyed the boat, looking for signs of damage. Water was bubbling up from beneath Randy's feet, but it didn't look too bad. With some luck, they may be able to make it to shore before taking on too much water. Part of Danny hoped that whatever that was had been an accident, that some sea creature had simply swam by and knocked into the boat, but in his lizard brain, the part of the brain that knew when a predator was near, he knew that to be false.

But that didn't explain why it had taken a bite of Randy's leg. Had that been mistaken identity? Danny knew sharks sometimes mistook surfers for seals, but they weren't surfing.

Another impact, again from directly underneath them. Somehow, the crack was louder than before, as if Heaven itself had been sundered. There was no questioning the extent of the damage this time; the kayak was taking on water at an alarming rate, and all hope of reaching the shore in it was lost.

Randy, barely conscious and still off balance from the impact, tumbled into the ocean. It happened so fast Danny barely registered his friend's blood-curdling scream.

Save Randy, or try to fix the kayak? From where Danny sat he wasn't sure he could do either of those things. He scanned the water immediately surrounding the kayak in search of his friend.

Just out of arm's reach, Danny spotted Randy doing his best to tread water, but it was clear that the loss of blood had done a number on him. If he didn't fall victim to whatever stalked the ocean, he would soon succumb to exhaustion and eventually drown. Only swift action could save Randy now, and Danny knew he couldn't live with himself if he tried fixing the kayak first.

There was only one choice as he saw it.

Danny reached for his friend, but he was too far. "You've gotta swim a little closer!" Danny shouted.

Randy did his best, better than Danny could have hoped, a little closer and he would be safe.

Their fingertips grazed.

Randy screamed once more before disappearing below the surface. The water where Randy had been turned a pinkish red and that awful color began spreading through the water. The sea made it difficult to tell, but Danny thought it looked like Randy was bleeding like a stuck pig this time.

A dorsal fin cut the surface of the ocean as a shark circled away from the bloody water. Danny was in a world of shit. He knew that now. From where he sat, he could see both the dorsal and caudal fins, and from what he saw, the fucking shark was massive.

It completed a 180-degree turn and the dorsal fin grew larger as the shark approached at a frightening speed. Death incarnate approached. Danny's bladder betrayed him. Warm piss ran down his leg at the realization a man-eating shark had attacked his friend and was coming back to finish the job. This was no mistaken identity. The shark had decided Randy was on the menu. And with the kayak taking on water the way it was, Danny might be the desert.

Despite the inevitable total failure of the kayak, Danny paddled like a mad man, maybe he could get close enough to shore he could swim back, or far enough from the beast that it wouldn't bother him when he eventually dove in the ocean.

For a moment, Danny's heart ached over the idea of leaving his friend. What if he wasn't dead yet? The mourning period was brief, as the moment the shark circled the perimeter of the sinking kayak, giving Danny a better view of the great hammerhead, self-preservation kicked in and Danny decided Randy was dead anyway, and he might as well utilize the distraction.

Impossible.

That was the only word he could think of to describe the shark. He was no marine biologist, but Danny knew for damn sure that great hammerhead's did not grow that large. He knew the species wasn't typically considered dangerous to humans, either. Though he supposed that any dangerous beast made exceptions from time to time.

But the size! This one had to be at least thirty feet, maybe more. It was larger even than any great white he'd ever heard of. Even more frightening, Danny knew hammerheads were widely considered to be among the smartest sharks in the ocean. He was up against the Albert Einstein of murdering marine life.

Wonderful.

Danny had known he was in trouble, but seeing the creature up close with his own two eyes hammered home precisely how well and truly fucked he was.

Fuck it, Danny thought. It was now or never. The kayak would go no further. He needed to make his move or accept his fate and wait for the shark to turn on him.

As he dove into the water, Danny's heart hammered in his chest, drowning out the sound of the UH-1N helicopter as it searched the ocean for two Marines who had been spotted at sea in direct violation of the base's restriction order.

Danny swam. He had no clue if the shark was coming for him. There was no doubt in his mind that the shark knew he was in the water. He knew enough about sharks to know that the predator had sensed him in the water the moment he'd jumped in. It didn't matter if the shark followed him or not; it wasn't like he had any other choice that he could think of. He could have tried clubbing it with a paddle, but that would have meant waiting for the kayak to sink enough to strand him in the water. There was no way he could generate the force necessary to even make the shark think twice if he had to swing the paddle through the water.

If only he still had the pocketknife, at least then he might be able to deter the shark, however unlikely that may be.

A few long minutes passed. They felt like hours. Danny was a skilled swimmer, but as fast as he was going, the men had taken the kayak so far from shore that it seemed to Danny like he had made no progress. The initial surge of adrenalin that fueled his struggle to reach shore could no longer hold back the exhaustion he felt in his body.

His labored breathing made the situation worse. Danny hadn't given enough thought to this part of the plan. Treading the ocean and hoping for a rescue was one thing, but attempting to do it after balls-to-the-wall swimming from a freak of nature hammerhead shark was something else entirely.

On a good day, he figured he could tread water for five maybe ten minutes at best. A special ops Marine he was not, and in fact, had failed the indoctrination exam after only being able to tread water for seven minutes. He hadn't been nearly as exhausted that day.

In short, the odds of survival were looking pretty fucking grim. Maybe he should give up now and let the sea claim him, rather than be eaten by a freak of nature.

His mind made up, Danny floated in place, waiting to

die. He thought he had already made peace with the fact he might die overseas, but until you come face to face with death, no man can say for sure that they really have accepted it.

He wept as the water washed over him, the waves crashing over his head. At the last moment, just before taking a lungful of the ocean, Danny panicked and realized he couldn't force himself to inhale the sea. He wanted to, but it takes more courage to kill yourself than he had considered.

"Grab the ladder," a voice yelled.

His mind, completely exhausted, had at last snapped. Another wave crashed against him, once again pushing him under the surface. When it had popped above sea level again, he thought he heard a voice again, but the thrumming of his pulse in his eardrums made it difficult to hear anything.

He opened his eyes in time to see the hammerhead fast approaching. *This is it*, he thought. *This is how it ends*.

Danny braced himself and put his arms out. He didn't know what he could do. He had no weapons. All he could do was try to grab onto the head of the creature and see if he could avoid its teeth. Maybe if this was a normal hammerhead, but the creature's head and mouth were much too large, and when he tried to do it, his hand slipped and the shark's teeth sliced his arm from mid-forearm to inner elbow. Blood poured from the wound, filling the ocean water around Danny. The shark swam in a wide arc, smelling and tasting the blood, no doubt fueling an insatiable appetite. After completing one more circle it would move in for the kill.

A ladder floated in the air, just a few feet from the surface of the water. Somehow, in all of the commotion,

Danny had failed to register the ladder and make out the voice calling to him.

"Grab the fucking ladder," the voice shouted again, hardly audible over the droning *whomp whomp whomp* of the helicopter blades.

Better late than never.

Danny hooked his arm around the ladder. The man hanging over the side reached down toward Danny, grabbing his wrist. The man squeezed, hard enough that Danny felt the bones grind. He began the arduous task of pulling Danny's battered body into the helicopter. Danny was too exhausted to be of much help.

The man pulling him into the helicopter had a balaclava covering his face. For what reason Danny couldn't say, but as he was yanked into the helicopter, he couldn't help but think that whoever this man was, he was a dickhead.

His rescuer gave the pilot a thumbs up gesture, and the helicopter flew from the scene.

"Man, when you get back to base, you're going to wish we never found you out here," said the man behind the mask.

"Who are you?"

"That's classified," the man laughed.

"How did you find me?"

Danny's rescuer spit out the side of the helicopter. "Stupid fucker was flying a drone on the beach, and saw your truck. Called it in to report it. Ended up dry snitching on himself that he was flying the drone over a no-fly zone. He won't be reporting much of anything for the foreseeable future."

"What do you mean?"

"Quiet, now," the masked man grabbed his M4A1 rifle

and butt-stroked Danny across the temple. Darkness stole his vision, and at last Danny rested.

———

DANNY WOKE UP, HIS BODY STILL EXHAUSTED. EVERY FIBER of every muscle felt as if it were lit aflame. He tried to stand but found the task beyond him. He couldn't even move his limbs, never mind get up. Looking down, the problem was immediately apparent—he was strapped to a steel chair in an otherwise spartan, sterile room. He fought against the restraints, and daggers of pain shot through his arm. The handcuffs were tight, biting his wrists. Something warm dripped down his forearm where the shark had bitten him.

"Be careful, you popped a stitch, Devil Dog," said a voice from behind the chair.

Danny heard the unmistakable click of corfam dress shoes as the voice behind him circled around him, stopping in front of Danny and revealing their identity.

The Marine Corps Base Hawaii commanding officer, Lt. Col. Merrigan.

Danny furrowed his brow. What was going on here? Despite his confusion, the respect for rank that had been drilled into him since boot camp took over. "Lieutenant Colonel Merrigan? Sir, I made a mistake. I shouldn't have gone into the water. I didn't realize I'd be put in the brig for this."

Lt. Col. Merrigan laughed. "Oh, PFC. Robinson, you're not going to the brig for the restriction. At most, that's an NJP. Nothing more than loss of rank and forfeiture of pay. No, you'll be getting court martialed for the murder of Lance Corporal Randy Ward. It seems upon responding to an SOS, the search and rescue operatives arrived on scene only to find you dumping poor Lance Corporal Ward's body parts into the ocean. You might have gotten away with it too, if it hadn't been for another Marine too stupid to follow orders."

"No, Lieutenant Colonel, that's not what happened. We got attacked by a massive shark. It was a hammerhead, bigger than anything I've ever seen before. It was a freak of nature, or an experiment gone wrong, or something. I don't know."

As soon as the words left his lips, Private First Class Danny Robinson knew he was right, or rather, that Randy's girlfriend had been right all along. The military *was* conducting experiments, after all. Danny bit his lip, shook his head.

"I can tell by the look on your face it's making a bit more sense, Marine." Lt. Col. Merrigan paced back and forth. "It is unfortunate, but we have come too far. Far too much money spent, ocean life destroyed, and human life wasted to let a couple of Marines not following orders ruin everything. Sadly, it falls to me to clean up this mess. I won't enjoy notifying Ward's family, but you've left me no choice. The results of the research here are truly something special. And the hammerhead is only the tip of the iceberg. In the end, your transgression worked out to our advantage. We were able to recover the hammerhead without the damn locals discovering the truth of what is going on here."

"My family won't believe it. There is no way you will get away with this!"

"It doesn't matter what your family believes, Robinson. They have no say over what goes on in a military trial. Unfortunately for you, I have plenty of influence. Have fun in the brig, Marine." Lt. Col. Merrigan did an about-face and marched out of the holding area, leaving Danny strapped to the chair.

Danny screamed for help that would never come. His escape from a watery grave had only delivered him to a life in the brig.

The death they'd promised him on a combat deployment overseas suddenly didn't seem so bad.

Cock-Meat Sandwich

Bleary-eyed, Robbie stumbled out of his bedroom and shambled down the hallway. He stopped at the end of the hallway. As he did every morning before heading downstairs, he reached up and placed his hand on the picture of his late wife and kids, the closest he would ever get to touching them again. Sighing, he took the stairs cautiously; he was utterly exhausted, and a broken neck before his morning coffee would not do.

He had been up all night, kept awake once again by the goddamn Gilroys. Robbie Harmon had moved to the sticks to avoid shit like this. Without a family to care for, he wanted no part of humanity. The Gilroys were the only neighbors for over a mile, and while, yes, their property lines were almost on top of each other, Robbie's property extended for acres in the other direction. When he had bought the home a few months ago, he wouldn't have believed having *one* neighbor could be so troublesome.

In the kitchen, the sun shone mockingly through Robbie's windows. Dust motes floated through the rays of sunbeam streaming in. Robbie didn't feel bright and cheery, but hoped that the sunshine, mixed with coffee and some breakfast could kickstart his day. Otherwise, he was well and truly fucked.

Robbie had expected to be greeted by the wonderful aroma of coffee brewing in his newly remodeled kitchen, but had discovered in his sheer exhaustion that although he had prepared the brew the night prior, he had forgotten to set the advance timer on the machine. Instead of the intoxicating aroma of Arabica beans, Robbie had to settle for the vomit inducing odor of dog shit.

Gary Gilroy and his fucked-up freakshow of a family didn't believe in pooper scoopers or putting the shit in bags; it seemed they believed in letting the rank animal feces fertilize the lawn. Judging by the grass growing shoulder height throughout most of their lawn, Robbie could only surmise that the shit was doing its job.

Sighing, Robbie walked over to the coffee pot and stabbed at the brew button. He was so exhausted he missed the button twice before finally hitting it, starting the brewing process. The pot turned on and immediately worked its magic. The wonderfully orgasmic smell hit his nostrils, perking him up ever so slightly. Hell, it *almost* overpowered the olfactory assault emanating from fecal landmines all over Gilroy's yard.

That was the final straw; nobody was going to ruin his morning coffee. Robbie was going to fuel up and then head over to the neighbors' house and give those inconsiderate pricks a piece of his mind.

———

ROBBIE DEVOURED A HALF DOZEN SCRAMBLED EGGS AND half of a package of bacon. He was starving, but still had to force himself to eat the food. Hungry as he was, he found it increasingly difficult to stomach anything of substance with the stench coming from the neighbors' house. After downing a pot of coffee and preparing another half pot—the first pot had hardly put a dent in his oppressive exhaustion—he threw some clean clothes on and exited the front door to his house, stomping his way to the neighboring property.

Robbie tried keeping to the walkway, but it made little difference when the grass was high enough he could have been using a machete to clear a path to the front door. Why take a trip to the jungle when you can visit the neighbor? He didn't want to think about what he might step on, or the parasites he might acquire on his trek through the shoulder-high grass. He would have to strip down and search for ticks the second he made it back to his place, Lyme disease wasn't on Robbie's bucket list.

Robbie jumped back in shock after stepping on something that offered a brief resistance before finally squelching beneath his foot. He wanted to tell himself it was dog shit, but he couldn't deny the death screams of whatever creature it had come from. With all the garbage in the yard, and the lawn being unkempt, it was likely a rat.

Fucking disgusting. He continued on the path and after what had seemed like ages, stood on the porch of the Gilroy residence.

If the property wasn't bad enough, the house itself was also a piece of shit. The type of dump that scares away potential neighbors. The peeling paint, mossy roof, and shingles broken and falling off the side of the house told you about all you needed to know about the Gilroys. It also went a long way to explaining why Robbie had been able to buy his house and the large lot it stood upon for so cheap. Hell, he had only bought it because after the violent death of his wife and children in a home invasion, Robbie never wanted to be found again. His new home had checked many of the boxes he needed to disappear forever. The only neighbor for as far as the eye could see doubled as the last neighbor you would ever *want* to see.

Straightening his shirt and wiping his palms on his sleeves, Robbie cleared his throat and pressed the doorbell. No dice.

Of course it doesn't work.

Robbie knocked. His frustration was getting the better of them, and he pounded the door harder than he intended to.

"Hold on, damnit!" a voice said from within.

The door opened a crack, and Robbie saw an eyeball peering at him from the narrow opening.

"Yes?" the voice that the eye belonged to asked.

"Ummm, hello, I'm Robbie Harmon. I live next door. Is Mr. Gilroy home?"

"Oh, Robbie, so you're the son of a bitch that called the cops on me when I was shooting my AK on my own damn property. You one of those liberal hippie sons-of-bitches that hate the constitution, are ya?"

Robbie scratched his head. "Yes. No. Wait, yes, I called the cops on you. I understand it's your property, but there's no need for it to sound like Afghanistan in the backyard at two=in-the-morning. No, I don't hate the constitution."

Gary swung the door open. "I oughtta skull fuck you for that one, you commie son-of-a-bitch."

"Listen, Mr. Gilroy, I don't want to be enemies. I want some courtesy. Your lawn is disgusting. It reeks of shit and garbage because you don't clean up after your dogs, and you use your backyard like it's the Johnston landfill."

Gilroy grabbed a disposable plate from the table next to his front door, peeled an object off of it, and took a bite.

Putrid juices smeared his lips as he gnashed away at the foul feast. Was that rotting meat? It stunk to high hell, and flies swarmed around the brown, festering mystery substance.

Gnashing his teeth, Gilroy took a hard swallow of whatever he had just bitten into before responding to Robbie. "Listen, shit stick, you're gonna want to get off my goddamn property before something unfortunate happens to you. And stay off the grass. You joke about Afghanistan, but the piles of dog shit aren't the only land mines in that there grass, boy."

Gilroy slammed the door in Robbie's face, ending the conversation as quickly as it started. Robbie thought he could hear Gilroy laughing over the sound of the deadbolt smacking home.

Fuming but not wanting to lose his cool and snap that old geezer's wrinkly, liver-spotted neck, Robbie stepped off the porch keeping his eyes focused on the ground. He didn't believe Mr. Gilroy booby-trapped his yard, but then again, the guy was clearly off his rocker. Who knew if he was bullshitting or not. Robbie didn't want to be the one to test those waters. Stepping on an explosive in a neighbor's yard, now that would be one for the record books.

Not like it mattered. He doubted he'd see anything in the yard with all of that grass, but he wasn't about to take a chance.

Robbie glanced back at the Gilroy house one last time and instantly regretted it.

Standing in the curtainless window, Mr. Gilroy stared at Robbie. The hatred emanating from that gaze pierced Robbie like daggers in his flesh. If that didn't make the situation uncomfortable enough, that Gary Gilroy was stark naked, holding the rancid meat he was still eating in one hand, while furiously stroking his own long, skinny meat with the other was downright stomach turning.

But that wasn't all. Gilroy brought the stinking, rotting meat down in front of his own throbbing meat. His face scrunched up, and Robbie swore the man was in the throes of orgasm.

Disgusted, but like a rubber-necker at a car wreck, Robbie could not walk away. It wasn't until Gilroy brought the cum-glazed meat up to his lips and took a massive bite that Robbie broke away. He lost his breakfast in Gilroy's overgrown lawn and ran home, shit and explosive land-mines be damned.

ANOTHER EVENING OF LITTLE TO NO SLEEP. THE GILROYS had thrown a banger of a party that went well into the early hours of the morning. Robbie tried to get rest, but sleep eluded him. Once midnight rolled around, Robbie had called the sheriff's department and found them to be little help. A combination of Covid staffing shortages along with the inability for law enforcement agencies to fill staffing vacancies countrywide had left night time response in their little town woefully inadequate. Local officers weren't coming out for overnight noise complaints, and the Rhode Island State Police certainly would not respond to such a complaint in the absence of local staffing. They had bigger fish to fry.

Robbie spent the morning guzzling mug after mug of coffee, to the point where he was genuinely concerned about his caffeine intake. Most of the vehicles that had been parked at the Gilroy residence had since vacated the premises, but there were a few beat down trucks parked on the grass. Robbie didn't know how some of those junk-boxes could run, never mind pass inspections to be on the road. If Robbie had to guess, they were being driven illegally.

Face still puffy with the woefully inadequate sleep he had gotten, Robbie got his household chores done early. He was going to take a brief road trip and flee town for a few days. He wasn't sure where, but he had vacation time to burn and a few nights in a hotel would likely provide a better sleep than the no sleep he was currently running on.

The droning sound of water flowing from the faucet made it difficult for Robbie to stay awake, tired as he was. The monotony of washing dishes was enough to put him to sleep even on days when he was well rested.

Sleep overtook Robbie, and his head drooped low for a moment before the action of the sudden movement snapped him awake. Back in his military days, they called that action "bobbing for cock."

The soapy dish slipped out of Robbie's hand, crashing into the sink and shattering into dozens of tiny, razor-sharp shards. "Goddamnit," he yelled.

Robbie was furious with himself for breaking a dish, but more so with the neighbors and their absolute inability to give the tiniest of fucks or consideration to anyone but themselves.

The smell of burning food penetrated Robbie's nostrils, briefly overtaking the smell of feces from the yard next door.

Robbie blinked his eyes, unable to comprehend the view from the window over his kitchen sink.

Mr. Gilroy, once again naked as the day he was born, stood beside his grill. Held in one hand, high above his head and slowly descending toward his gaping maw was what appeared to be a severed, char-grilled penis. Mr. Gilroy dropped the long, genital sausage in his mouth and chewed the delicacy as his free hand savagely finger-banged the ragged, bloody hole where his cock had once been with an intensity of motion that jiggled his man-tits and flabby skin.

Robbie would have laughed at the sight of the man's saggy breasts flapping if it weren't for the incomprehensible horror of what he was watching.

Mr. Gilroy wiped the cooked cock juices off his chin and locked eyes with Robbie, pointing at him and laughing.

Robbie didn't know what the fuck that was about, and he sure as shit didn't want to find out. He closed the blinds over the sink, picked up his cell, and dialed 911.

After explaining what he had just witnessed, the 911 operator informed him of laws regarding prank calling emergency services before she cut the connection, leaving Robbie in silence.

He looked out the window again.

Mr. Gilroy was gone.

A crash at the front door stole his attention.

Robbie grabbed the biggest knife from the butcher block and crept through the kitchen. He hoped he didn't have to use it, but after what he just witnessed, he knew that was wishful thinking. Someone wasn't leaving this house unscathed, and Robbie wasn't inclined to be murdered by some freakshow in the comfort of his own home.

Crossing the threshold from the kitchen to the main hall, not a soul was around. The front door hung limply on broken hinges. The chain had snapped, but in his exhaustion, Robbie had forgotten to engage the deadbolt, something he did religiously since his family's death.

This motherfucker kicked the door that hard? Barefoot?

Robbie slipped by the door, careful not to touch it for

fear of alerting Gilroy to his current positioning. He peeked his head around the door quickly, making sure Gilroy wasn't outside.

Nobody there.

Robbie continued on through the house and entered the den. The television was off, as he had left it. Nothing looked out of place.

Thud.

Gilroy must have bumped into an end table in the hallway. Robbie turned around and snuck his way around the other side of the den, exiting into the hallway from the rear doorway of the den. He poked his head around the corner; still nothing.

A creak from the kitchen.

Moving swiftly and silently, Robbie stalked his way back to the kitchen. As he entered, he saw Gilroy sitting at his dining table. Gilroy was placing a hotdog bun on a disposable paper plate.

Robbie charged at Gilroy, knife overhead, hoping to frighten him into retreating.

Gilroy, with a speed that could only be described as uncanny, hopped off the chair and in one smooth motion, rolled something across the floor. Robbie was blinded with tunnel vision, and although he saw Gilroy jump up, he *did not* see the severed scrotum slick with blood and viscous fluid rapidly roll across the floor.

Robbie stepped on the bloody ball bag and his foot flew out from under him, sending him flat on his back. His head smacked the hardwood floor, and he saw stars flitting across his vision. Robbie tried to get to his feet, but was too dazed to do so quickly.

In a flash, Gilroy stood over him and swung a large hunk of wood.

Crack. The wood splintered into hundreds of tiny pieces.

Darkness overtook Robbie.

———

A THROBBING PAIN IN HIS GROIN RIPPED ROBBIE FROM THE darkness that had swallowed him. He awoke to the smell of meat cooking. Bit by bit, his vision came back as his kitchen replaced the blackness that had enveloped him.

Something sizzled in a skillet, but Robbie could remember putting nothing on the stovetop. He tried to walk to the stove so he could turn it off, but couldn't move.

"What the fuck?" Robbie looked down and discovered the problem. He was bound to a chair by heavy duty nylon rope. A portable, wooden food tray rested on his lap. Something between his legs burned, but Robbie couldn't see anything below the tray.

"What the fuck indeed," Gilroy stepped in front of Robbie's field of vision and held up a syringe. "You've been out for some time. I may have used too much ketamine. I wasn't sure how long that log would have you out for; couldn't risk you waking too soon."

Robbie stared in horror at Gilroy as he suddenly remembered how he had ended up tied to a chair. The man was off his rocker even more than Robbie had thought.

Gilroy was still naked, dried blood had crusted to his inner thighs, and the ragged hole where his cock had been was no longer bleeding; instead, the wound was freshly charred.

Gilroy held up a handheld torch. "Don't worry, I had enough fuel left to cauterize the both of us."

"Cauterize… what?"

Gilroy smiled, revealing a mouthful of broken and discolored teeth. He lifted the tray from Robbie's lap, unveiling the gruesome scene.

As he realized the cause of pain between his legs, Robbie looked at his groin and screamed. Robbie was now as cockless as Gilroy, and had the ragged, cauterized hole to match. Robbie's screams turned to sobs, and he failed to formulate words.

Gilroy returned the tray to its resting place on Robbie's lap. He snatched the plate off the table and sauntered over to the skillet. Whistling while he worked, Gilroy turned the burner off, picked up a set of tongs and picked up the cooked mystery meat, moving the meat from the skillet to the hotdog bun.

"Do you like ketchup on your cock, Robbie?" Gilroy squirted a hearty helping of ketchup onto the cock-dog, the bottle farting as he squeezed.

Robbie fought and screamed, but the ropes were too tight. There was no give.

Gilroy brought the sandwich to Robbie's mouth. "Open wide."

Robbie held his mouth closed as Gilroy stuffed the cock to his lips. No way he was eating his own Johnson.

Gilroy smiled, and with his free hand, pinched Robbie's nose closed.

Robbie held his breath for as long as he could, but his lungs betrayed him and as they burned for oxygen, his mouth shot open, gasping for air.

Gary Gilroy seized the moment and stuffed the cock-dog in Robbie's mouth, pushing it deep into Robbie's throat, forcing him to deepthroat his own penis.

Robbie's eyes bulged. The grisly meal blocked his airway, preventing him from breathing.

He tried to chew his cock and swallow, but the bulk of

his own member was lodged in his throat. Robbie's meat muffled his screams, and his fruitless struggle achieved nothing more than using up the last of his rapidly dwindling supply of oxygen.

Purple faced and fading fast, Robbie could do nothing but watch as Gilroy showed himself out, leaving Robbie to choke on his cock-meat sandwich in the solitude he had so badly wanted.

Bow Saw

"*A trash bag containing human remains was discovered inside a dumpster behind a local Cranston hardware store. Although authorities claim it as the fourth discovery of its kind this year, a source inside the Cranston Police Department has revealed to me the actual number is much higher. The same source has also told Channel 12 there are no tangible leads.*"

Leslie Moranis turns the television off. "Sick fucks, all of them," she says. Her phone pings and a notification flashes across the screen. It's Travis, her latest Tinder discovery. God, she hates that app. If she comes across one more picture of some jackass holding a fish up for the camera, she is going to lose her shit.

Leslie swipes up and opens Tinder.

Hey sexy. R U Ready for tonight? The message reads.

Leslie rolls her eyes. *Ready and waiting, Trav.*

Three dots appear, another message incoming from Travis. *Daddy is going to fill you up,* followed by an eggplant emoji.

Leslie tosses the phone on the table. She refuses to dignify that bullshit with a response. Yeah, she's on this hookup app for a reason, but that kind of bullshit is liable to drive anyone insane. Let the dipshit sit on read for a while, keep him guessing. The magic of these apps is that, just like meeting a man at a bar, they want one thing and one thing only.

Pussy.

She could ignore the stupid fuck, never respond again, and in the end he would still show up at her door with the pizza, the drinks, and the condoms. Because if he didn't, he had zero hopes of getting laid. Men want pussy. They would put up with whatever necessary to get their dick wet. It's a scientific fact. On Tinder, there are hundreds of prospective men for her to choose from at any given moment, whereas he likely only had a few dozen prospects.

Leslie crosses her studio apartment—a small, yet tidy place—opens her tiny refrigerator and pulls out a box of sangria. Typically, she liked to be sober when her dates arrived, but Travis is a special kind of stupid, and sees no issue indulging.

Leslie drinks the glass of sangria in one long chug. She puts the glass down and considers it for a moment before she pours herself another. Travis wouldn't be over for a bit. Leslie has more than enough time to get ready.

Hey sexy. R U Ready for tonight? Travis types.

Ready and waiting, Trav. Leslie's response.

Travis feels the blood rush from his big head to his little head and responds. *Daddy is going to fill you up.*

He is about to hit send but stops and adds an eggplant emoji. The *coup de grâce* if you will. These Tinder women are after the same thing he is. The only difference is they *pretend* they want more. They play the game. But really, if they did, why are they on Tinder? It's been around long enough that everyone knows you go on Tinder for sex, not love. So Travis lets them play their game, because in the end they are running for the same finish line.

Travis puts his phone in his pocket, not waiting for a response. He's already picked up the pizza and the drinks. A box of sangria for the lady, just in case she's out, and a bottle of Knob Creek for the gentleman.

Travis hates to be late. Well, he hates to be later than the five minutes planned lateness. He *always* shows up five minutes late, and can't imagine showing up on time. It's ok to be desperate, hell the girls *know* you're desperate for what they've got. The key to dropping their panties lies in one simple rule. Feign indifference. Once they know they've got you wrapped around their finger, they no longer want you.

Travis cranks up the volume in his 4Runner. He's got some time to spare, might as well get in the mood.

———

Leslie hikes her leggings up. The new "booty" leggings everyone is buying from amazon. She turns and sticks her ass out to the mirror. Yeah, the leggings do the advertised job. Certified dumpy. More and more men were "ass-men" these days, which plays to Leslie's strength. She's no slouch in the back, but the leggings add an extra pop. She might as well be wearing body paint.

A knock at the door. Leslie jumps. It's almost time. She's jittery. After all, she had invited a stranger into her home. Anything could happen. It's thrilling, really. Russian roulette. Give me dick or give me death. Leslie laughs at that thought and makes her way to the front door. Using the camera app on her phone, she checks her reflection one last time. Everything is on point, and she is absolutely sure Travis is going to give her exactly what she craves. Leslie locks her phone and opens the door.

———

Travis knocks on the door five minutes late, according to plan. If things continue according to the plan, Travis knows it will be a long night. Rocking back and forth on his heels, Travis waits for Leslie to answer his summon. It's taking longer than he would like. Nobody makes Travis wait.

The longer I wait, the harder I'm going to give it to her. This thought crosses his mind, coinciding with the shit-eating grin smeared across his face. The door opens. The grin vanishes.

Damn, she's stacked. Taller than I thought, too. She's a gym rat, for sure.

Travis flashes a welcoming smile at Leslie. A gesture meant to charm and put her at ease. "Leslie, it's nice to finally meet you," Travis says.

"Nice to meet you, too," Leslie replies. "Now let's hope you can do more than talk a big game."

She spins and walks away, Travis follows, eyes glued to the finest ass he has ever laid eyes upon.

———

Leslie grabs Travis by the hand, leads him to the bed in the center of her studio apartment. At the edge of the bed they stop and Travis grabs her by the hips. He tries bending her over, but Leslie resists. This is her territory, and she's in control.

Leslie turns to Travis, licking her lips. Grabbing his

shoulders, she spins him around and pushes him to the bed. The heat of the moment consumes her, and soon she's on her knees, pulling his pants around his ankles. She takes him in her mouth. Tonight will be a special night. For both of them.

———

TRAVIS STANDS OVER THE TOILET, SHAKES THE LAST droplets of post coitus piss from his cock. He flushes the toilet and washes his hands in the sink. His reflection in the vanity mirror catches his eye. His face is still flush from the hard fucking. Travis is happy with his performance, which left Leslie passed out on the bed.

He opens the vanity cabinet. "Wonder what's in here?" Travis says. He knows he shouldn't snoop, but he doesn't care. This is a wham, bam, thank you ma'am. He has no intent on seeing Leslie again.

Disappointed with the contents of the cabinet, Travis closes the mirror.

He jumps.

There's a reflection behind his own. Leslie is standing there, silent, like a fucking weirdo. The vacant look in her eyes worries him.

Caught in the act, he tries laughing it off. Tries to explain himself. "I was just looking for…"

Travis feels a flash of pain against the base of his skull. It doesn't last long; darkness takes hold of him before he crumples to the floor.

———

LESLIE GRUNTS. SHE'S EXHAUSTED FROM THE SEX, AND HER body is groggy from booze. She winces at the crunch

Travis's skull makes when he drops to the ground, his skull smashing the side of the toilet bowl. No need to worry about him waking up. Leslie leaves the bathroom, walks to the front closet and retrieves a bag from the local hardware store. She returns to the bathroom and removes a bow saw from the bag. In hindsight, dropping off the trash in that dumpster had been a good idea. She had needed a new saw.

Leslie places the saw against the meat of his shoulder and works the saw back and forth. The task at hand is difficult, but something she has grown accustomed to. Blood spews forth with each push and pull of the saw. She continues the work until Travis is an amputee.

Leslie tries to wipe the blood and sweat from her eyes, but she is covered head to toe. She makes a mental note to buy goggles on her next trip to the hardware store, her eyes sting from getting blood in them. It's a process, one she has yet to perfect. But she will, eventually. There are plenty of men, and plenty of time to refine.

———

LESLIE PULLS AROUND THE BACK OF WILEY'S TRU-VALUE. It's early. The sun has yet to rise. She gets out of her Toyota Avalon, walks around the car and pops the trunk. The hefty bag is heavy, so she thinks maybe she should have put the parts in a few different bags, spread them in different dumpsters. Less physical work for her, and it may be a fun game to play with the detectives. Food for thought, with the way the investigation is going. Leslie thinks so long as she doesn't slip up, she will have plenty of time.

"A lot of sick fucks around here," she says as she looks at her watch. Wiley's doesn't open for another few hours, plenty of time to take off with no witnesses around. She can smell the McDonald's across the street. Did someone inside the restaurant see her? She doesn't know. Her stomach rumbles. She wants a breakfast sandwich, but isn't so bold as to dine so close to her dumping ground.

A notification pings her phone. She pulls it out. Another Tinder cock, another unoriginal message.

Hey bb WYD.

Leslie pockets the phone. This one has potential.

Noose

Dear Chuck,

First off, let me apologize in advance. As a coworker and a friend, what I'm going to leave you with is wrong. I don't know how to start something like this, and I don't know if it's possible to prove or disprove if what I'm experiencing is real or not. All I can do is leave you with what I understand to be the truth. For that, we start with the breakdown of my marriage.

I had stormed out the front door of my home for the last time, slamming it closed hard enough that the latch failed to catch. The door rattled the frame and swung open. I didn't stop, couldn't make myself look back. It wouldn't have mattered. Nobody followed me. Nobody bothered to stop me. I hopped into my Toyota Tacoma and pushed the ignition start button. What a waste of money. I spent six-thousand dollars more for a higher trim level, not because I needed any of the bells and whistles, but because I wanted a push to start button. I didn't want to turn my key in the ignition like some kind of peon. I learned then that life is nothing more than a sequence of horrible decisions strung together. Well, my life, anyway. Decisions like marrying a tinder date within a year of meeting. Decisions made with the head between my legs rather than the one attached to my neck. One day, I was holding my baby, living the American Dream, and the next I was walking out the door of my home, knowing that in a few hours some other dude would walk in that same door.

With the push of a button, my truck's engine roared to life. The cold air intake and aftermarket exhaust had given it an unmistakable growl. Yeah, I know what you're going to say, Chuck, "What kind of tool does that to a Tacoma?" Me. I'm the tool, now get out of my fucking head and let me write this. Anyway, something in the truck stunk like shit. I rolled the windows down, hoping the scent of excrement would drift out the window and leave me in peace. Still driving, I picked up my phone and, using my one free hand, scrolled through my music library looking for the perfect soundtrack to frame my anger. I selected the new As I Lay Dying album and turned the volume up. The guitar riffs assaulted my eardrums. I inhaled deep and let the cool, night air fill my lungs. I shifted the transmission into drive and pressed the pedal to the floor. The tires squealed and the truck shot forward, leaving a trail of rubber and smoke in its wake. Yeah, I was a jackass, but I was a *pissed off* jackass. After a few minutes, I eased off the gas and merged onto I-95.

Driving north with no destination in mind, I brought the truck to a felonious speed. The white painted lines on the highway separating lanes registered as nothing more than a blur on the asphalt. A speeding ticket was the least of my worries. As much as I would feel like a piece of shit if it came to it, I wouldn't hesitate to ask for professional courtesy. Sometimes pulling the Correction Officer card worked. Other times, it was a sure-fire way to get your ass thrown in the back of a car. Was it wrong to ask for that courtesy? Yep. Did I care? Nope. I continued driving until my heart rate had returned to normal and the throbbing in my temple subsided.

A profound sadness replaced the anger I felt. My grip on the steering wheel relaxed as a wave of grief swept over me, threatening to drown me in its high tide. I was all over the place emotionally, and I had every reason to be. It's not every day you find out your wife was having her cake and eating it too.

My wife's infidelity consumed my focus, and I stopped paying attention to my surroundings until I noticed the stench of human excrement had returned. Despite the open windows, the funk had somehow gotten worse. It was coming from inside the cab of my truck, that was for sure. But where? Did that bitch throw a dirty diaper in the back seat before I left? Was it me? I was an emotional wreck, sure, but I felt like it would have been difficult to shit myself and not realize it, and I wasn't unclean. Hygiene was still a part of my daily routine. I wasn't *that* much of a wreck. At least not yet.

I turned my head to the right and searched for the source of the odor. It was then that I locked eyes with a corpse. I know, it sounds crazy, but there was a dead fucking body riding shotgun. Its eyes bulged from their sockets. A bloated, dry tongue hung from the side of a drooping mouth. The stiff's face was pale; Pallor mortis had set in. Ligature marks were visible on its neck. What the fuck was a dead man doing in my truck? I screamed like a newborn, and, in a panic, cut the wheel to the left, steering my brand new truck straight into a fucking jersey barrier.

The following morning, I woke up in a hospital bed. The man's face was still fresh in my mind. It was familiar, but different. I know that makes no sense, but don't try to tell me you've never seen a person you swore to high heaven that you knew, but didn't know how you knew them. This was that feeling, I knew the man, but I didn't know how. Not that it mattered. There was no way I saw what I thought I saw. I must have spaced out and had some kind of stress-induced hallucination. The doctor confirmed my suspicions when she told me I had fallen asleep at the wheel. I'm not sure if I *should* be relieved that I was in such an emotionally exhausted state that I was capable of falling asleep at the wheel, but the flip side of that coin was the appearance of an obese ghost who'd hung himself. Not really jazzed about option A or option B, if I'm being honest.

As I was being discharged, the nurse overseeing my care handed me a plastic bag containing my clothes. Turns out I really had shit in my pants! Further proof that the corpse existed only in my mind.

Or so I convinced myself.

I'd like to sit here and tell you everything got better, but as the saying goes, I only have my balls and my word.

I would, instead, become obsessed with my wife's affair. Sure, we were getting a divorce, but we hadn't even filed the initial paperwork yet, and it went straight up my ass that her affair was going on in my home, in the presence of my child while I slept on a fucking twin size bed at my father's house. For months, I drove by our home after work. There was no need to do this. If anything, it contributed to the steady decline of my mental health, but it was like staring at a car wreck. I couldn't help myself.

Visits with my son had been few and far between. I wanted to be with him as much as possible, but unfortunately, I was also stuck paying the mortgage and all the bills in a home I no longer lived in, which meant that on the days my son stayed with me, my parents had to babysit while I went to work. Still the family's lone source of income, I had to continue working upwards of thirty hours of overtime per week. That is, until the divorce finalized. After that, who knows what the court would decide as far as alimony. The only certainty, according to my lawyer, was that I'd be on the hook for anywhere between twelve to fourteen hundred dollars a month in child support. For one child! I laughed when he told me that, because how the fuck was I supposed to afford a place for myself? A vasectomy seemed like an excellent idea for the future.

Work wasn't the only thing keeping me from my boy either. My sanity was slipping, and I was aware that I might have been losing my fucking mind. Scratch that— that fucker had left the building. Remember the dead guy in my truck? Yeah, he's back. ALL. THE. FUCKING. TIME. Check this out. One night while I was alone at my father's house, in the dead of night I woke up freezing my balls off. My nipples were hard enough to cut holes through the sheets. I got up to take a piss because it was 2:30 a.m. and I have the bladder of a five-year-old. There was no way in hell I was going to be able to fall back asleep without relieving myself. I stumbled to the bathroom, bumping into everything in my path because I was three sheets to the wind. I hadn't gone a night without hitting a bottle of Knob Creek since the piece of shit I used to call a life got flushed down the toilet. With battered shins and a broken toenail, I arrived at the porcelain god, ready to make a spiritual deposit. I let loose the golden stream, pulled my shorts back up, and washed my face in the sink. Yes, I washed my hands first, I'm not a fucking animal.

I wish I had never looked into the mirror that night.

The dead man's reflection replaced my own.

I stumbled backward and tripped over the bathroom

scale. My first thought was that I was hallucinating again, and I really needed to lay off the bourbon.

I scrambled to my feet and looked back at the mirror. The oval glass hanging over the sink pulsed like a heart suffering from tachycardia. I watched wide-eyed as the glass stretched outward. It had been like something straight out of *A Nightmare on Elm Street*. Whatever the fuck this thing was, it was coming out of the bathroom mirror. I could only hope it wasn't the dream demon himself. Thank god I already took a piss, otherwise I'd have soiled myself. Again.

I know what comes next in those types of movies, so I turned around and hauled ass down the hallway, taking the stairs two at a time. The sound of the mirror shattering, and shards of glass raining down into the sink, encouraged me to keep moving. I swiped my truck keys off the countertop and sped toward the front entrance. Thank God the body shop had completed the repairs only a few days before and I had the truck back, because something grabbed my shoulder, squeezing it hard enough to stop me in my tracks. I yanked my arm back with enough force to free myself from its grasp.

"Save me," it said. Its voice was horrible. The sound of the grave. A wet, garbled sound. That must be what people mean when they say a *death rattle*.

To the dismay of my spectral stalker, the only motherfucker I planned on saving was myself. I got my ass back in gear and jumped behind the wheel of my truck, peeling tires and speeding away in a matter of seconds. I know what you're going to say—I shouldn't have been drinking and driving. Well, no shit, Sherlock, but if my choice is death or DUI, I'm taking the DUI. At least that selection isn't a guaranteed death, so long as I didn't crash again. After a quick trip, I parked my truck in the parking lot of a nearby 24-hour chain store and tried to sleep it off.

The sunrise pried me away from the grip of sleep. If you could even call it sleep after consuming as much alcohol as I had the previous night. The effects of the liquor were still ravaging my body, but I needed to go home. I couldn't just stay in a parking lot all day, even though I was terrified and wanted to. Luckily, the sun's light has a funny way of pushing the terrors of the night to the background of the mind, leaving enough room for a man's stupidity to break through. I pulled into the driveway and shifted the truck into park. Sitting in the driveway, I had to once again steel my nerves and work myself to get out of the car. It's easy to lose your spine when you return to the scene of something like whatever I had experienced last night. Getting out of the truck, I left the motor running. Better safe than sorry. I crept through the house, stretching my senses to the height of human capabilities. It pains me to say it, but I had wished my father was home. At least I wouldn't be in the house alone. When I reached the top of the stairs, I stopped and gathered my nerves. Was I being haunted, or was I hallucinating?

I crossed the hallway and entered the bathroom.

Shards of broken glass littered the sink and covered the bathroom floor.

I'm a train wreck, in case you haven't figured that out yet. I'm suffering from addiction issues, self-destructive behaviors, anger problems, and severe depression. Have I told you I don't know what's real and what isn't anymore? If you haven't been able to pick that tidbit of knowledge up from reading this note, I'll spell it out for you. I don't. I'd love to believe I'm hallucinating. Imagine being at a point in your life where you *want* to believe that you're *just* hallucinating. Maybe I'm dead? And this is purgatory? That would explain a lot, I guess. Actually now that I think about it, it makes sense. At least it would explain the dead guy following me around everywhere. The bathroom incident was the last time my friend appeared in such a horrific manner, but he hasn't forgotten about me. I can feel him. Always in the back of my mind. You can sense when someone is near you. I get that feeling all the time now. Like if I turn around I'll catch a glimpse of him. But who is he? How do I save him? Is that really what he wants? I mean, I heard it the other night, but maybe it's a trap. And why me? All I know is this has been ongoing for weeks, and I'm ready for it to end. It's tiring.

When I had finally reached my wits end, he vanished. I don't mean like ghost vanished, mind you. He simply stopped appearing. I'm not sure when I stopped seeing him; I just remember feeling like it had been a while. Maybe if I stopped drinking long enough for the alcohol to stop influencing my mind I'd be able to remember important shit like that. But I must be going blind, because I can't see myself getting sober. Get it? I can't *see* myself getting sober… Fuck you, Chuck, you never did have a sense of humor. Let me make light of the situation. I'm just trying to have a bit of fun here at the end. As I said, the ghost was gone, for now at least. I felt as if a weight had suddenly been lifted from my shoulders.

I was free.

Boy was I wrong.

He paid me a visit at work. And he showed me everything I needed to know. What I've known this whole time but refused to see.

I arrived at work about fifteen minutes early tonight with my "tough guy" water container in tow. The funny thing about this giant container of water—there isn't a drop of water to be found. I've discovered work is far more tolerable when I fill it with whiskey and Coke. I shouldn't drink on the job, but I really don't care anymore. Also, that's beside the point. Let me get back on track. Once I assumed my post, I conducted the nightly inventory check and then knocked back a few more swigs from my jug. Before long, I felt a good buzz coming on and I just knew that tonight would be a good night. Come to find out, my buddy had other plans for me. The first few hours went by about as routine as you could hope in a prison. Hell, even the cockroaches and mice were quiet tonight.

Until the 2:30 a.m. check.

I hate the 2:30 a.m. check.

By this point of the night, I'm always exhausted. The graveyard shift really does a number on you. So, I'm doing my thing, walking from cell to cell, shining my light in the window. Gotta make sure everyone's still alive, you know? As I made it to cell twelve, I peered into the tiny sliver of a window, and it's like disco fucking fever in there, man. Maintenance still hasn't fixed the damn light even though I've put the request in every night for the last month. In between the flickers of illumination, I saw someone hanging. I cried out in surprise and fell flat on my ass.

Shit.

The last thing I needed was to have a suicide attempt in my area while I'm cocked. I rose to my feet and a few of the inmates laughed at me. Why sleep when you can call the officer things like "fatass" and "the blob". And yeah, maybe they were right. I put on some weight, but I've been going through a lot lately. I can still see my dick when I piss, so there's that, at least. Well, technically I can. But only in the morning if I've got morning wood when I take a leak.

Back to my original point. There was no mistaking it,

there was a motherfucker hanging. He had a sheet tied around his hands on one end, and his ankles at the other end. A second sheet was tied around his neck at one end, with the other end tied around the far side of the top bunk. Leaning forward would allow gravity to asphyxiate him while the sheet around his ankles would prevent him from changing his mind. The idea, while simple in design, worked perfectly. I was about to call the suicide in over the radio, but as I keyed the talk button, the hairs on the back of my neck stood at attention.

Nobody was assigned to cell twelve. Cell twelve was red tagged for use until maintenance could resolve the lighting issue. Rather than making a fool of myself on the radio (and bring attention to the fact I was drinking on the job), I decided to check it out one more time. I ran back to the control center, grabbed a cutting tool from the inventory rack, and pressed the unlock button on the control panel for cell twelve. I arrived at the cell as the sliding door finished opening. That smell was back, the one from my truck. Shit and decaying flesh. The combination of liquor and horrific stench almost forced me to puke. I choked back the burning contents of my stomach and entered the cell.

Plain as day, someone was hanging, but definitely not an inmate. The man was wearing an officer's uniform. My first thought was that a coworker decided he couldn't take it anymore, and rather than off himself at home, leaving a body for his family to discover, he decided to do the deed at work. After all, it wouldn't be the first time someone found a man hanging in a prison. I grabbed the man by the waist and lifted. If I could relieve pressure on his neck, maybe I could save him. It was useless. He was already dead. I knew that, but it was a habit from training for this exact situation.

I struggled with the weight of his gelatinous blob of a body, barely keeping him secure while I lifted the blade to the sheet and cut. As I did so, he grabbed me by my wrist and squeezed. A sharp pain radiated through my hand as the bones ground against one another.

"You can't save me anymore," he croaked, and with a strength I've never seen, flinging me across the cell like a fucking rag doll. Or maybe not; maybe I tripped. I'm too drunk to separate fact from fiction. All I know is that my head smacked against the concrete and I struggled to stay awake, my vision swimming back and forth between consciousness and all-consuming darkness. I clawed my way back to reality and stood up.

I stared him right in the eyes.

The eyes were familiar.

They were my own.

I don't understand how such a thing is possible, but then again, does anyone understand what really happens when we die? Now that I realized that the ghost haunting me was none other than my own ghost, it started to make sense. As much sense as a time traveling ghost could make anyway. The best I could figure was that in the future, I would kill myself, and that my ghost went back in time to warn me of my own impending doom. I was trying to save myself.

They say twenty-two veterans a day kill themselves. Studies also show one in every three correction officers suffer from PTSD and depression. When my marriage fell apart, I had a choice. I could pick myself up and press on, or I could become another statistic.

I continued staring at my corpse. The pallid color of death on its skin was a stark contrast to the vibrancy of my own living body. Under the beard, under all that fat, was my own defeated face. It looked exactly as I do now. I had really let myself go these last few months. I wish I saw it sooner. I wish someone had helped me. It's ok though, I'm not worried anymore. I haven't been a father to my son since everything turned to shit, and frankly, with my pension and savings in his name, I might be worth more to him dead than alive.

Confronted with the knowledge of my eventual fate, I fled the cell and returned to the control center. The least I could do was pick a pen up and leave an explanation.

Chuck, my man, I'm going to miss seeing you here in the mornings. I wish we could talk more. It would have been nice to get to know my partner better. It's not your fault, as I've been a complete mess and was the one who refused to reach out before it was too late. I mentioned this earlier, but again, I'm sorry to leave something like this for you to deal with at the start of the shift. I'll leave the cutting tool on top of the clipboard; you're going to need it.

BEST WISHES,
　　Steve Dipetro

<u>Wing Night</u>

elp Me!
Patrick pressed the end button on his phone, disconnecting the call. He looked around, searching for the voice that shouldn't be there. Maybe it had just been crossed signals on the cell tower. It happened, especially times when the weather was rough. Times such as tonight, the first real thunderstorm of the year. The local weather commission had sent severe weather advisories out, but really there was nothing to do but stay inside and hope you didn't lose power.

Patrick wasn't worried about a loss of power. One perk of the temporary living arrangement that he had with his friend Sean was that money solved a lot of problems. Sean's dad had purchased an entire house generator a few years back, a fact that Mr. Butler was very proud of, and told anyone who listened at the first opportunity to do so.

No, the thing that worried Patrick this evening was a twenty-five minute wait for his goddamn wing delivery to show up. Patrick was fucking starving, and felt as if he would pass out at any moment if he didn't eat. He hated to be that prick that ordered food with the weather being what it was this evening, but he needed to eat, and hadn't gone grocery shopping. When the father and son Butler duo had left for their family reunion, they had given him some money for his own trip to his Aunt Rita's house in Cape Cod. The problem was, Aunt Rita didn't exist. Patrick had lied because he wished to stay home, having no desire to spend time with the extended Butler clan. Sean's dad wouldn't have allowed it however, so Patrick fabricated a story about an aunt from the cape.

Cash in hand and nobody to answer to, Patrick had bought weed with the money, rather than food and spent the afternoon getting high and sleeping on the couch.

A massive, booming blast of thunder had ripped him from his nap, almost causing him to shit himself. By the time the cobwebs cleared from his brain enough to realize the cabinets were bare, the only market in walking distance had already closed for the evening, leading Patrick to use the remaining cash on takeout.

Parkside Wings To Go had the best wings in town, and while the wait would be excruciating, it would certainly be worth it. Patrick was salivating at the mere thought of those boneless nuggets from heaven. He'd ordered two pounds of wings. Unable to decide between buffalo or honey barbecue—both flavors were to die for—he did what any self-respecting 17-year-old pothead would do: he'd ordered both. As a bonus, his friend, Haik, was working tonight and had applied an employee discount to the order.

Lightning flashed across the sky with another blast of thunder hot on its heels.

Patrick jumped and dropped his phone on the floor, snapping the flip screen off of the receiver. "You've got to be fucking kidding me."

The storm was too close for comfort, and although Patrick was happy to have the house to himself for the weekend, that didn't make being home alone in the middle of the woods during a thunderstorm any less frightening. Seventeen was still a child, no matter how much Patrick hated to admit it.

In the basement, a buzzer sounded. Patrick's clothes were finished drying. He hated the basement, especially at night. It was common knowledge that the Butler residence was haunted. Many times throughout their childhood the neighborhood kids had backed out of sleepovers, citing the ghosts of children crying out in the basement.. And while Patrick himself had heard nothing, at least two of his close friends to this day still refused to be caught dead at the Butler residence after the sun went down, petrified of what they may hear, or worse, see.

Though Patrick had no paranormal experiences to speak of, the basement creeped him out. The mere thought of being in the basement while he was home alone left a feeling of dread in the pit of his stomach that puckered his asshole and made his balls feel as if they had re-ascended into his body. He was half tempted to leave the clothes in the dryer until the morning, but he expected the Butlers to arrive early, and if he overslept and Sean's father came home before he had removed the clothes there would be hell to pay.

The last time Patrick left his clothes in the dryer for a few hours after the cycle finished, Sean's father, Bobby, had gone downstairs to do his own laundry, and in the process had discovered the travesty of Patrick's clothes left unfolded in the dryer.

The man had damn near blown a gasket. Bobby had threatened to snatch up all of Patrick's belongings in a trash bag and toss them, along with Patrick, out on his ass if he were to so much as think about making the mistake of inconveniencing him again. Not a scenario he wanted to revisit.

If all went according to plan, Patrick wouldn't be an inconvenience in anyone's life much longer. He'd had enough of feeling like a burden, and as soon as he graduated high school, he would enlist in the Marine Corps. But for the time being, he was forced to leech off the charity of the Butler family. At least the school year was almost finished.

Bobby Butler had wanted no part of letting Patrick stay in his home for the year. Patrick had overheard enough of those conversations on numerous occasions to know that Sean's father could give two shits about Patrick; he had simply grown tired of the incessant nagging that he suffered at the hands of his son daily until he had finally relented.

Patrick's parents had lost their home halfway through his senior year. The house had caught fire, but a snafu with the insurance company left them homeless. The snafu being that Patrick's parents had let the insurance lapse, spending the money on drugs, and when his father had passed out in a crack induced haze, the cigarette that torched the house had also sent Patrick's future up in flames.

For as long as Patrick could recall, things at his own home had always been less than ideal, which he supposed was the norm when your father was a crackhead and your mother sucked and fucked the neighborhood dads to pay the mortgage. It was always a treat at school to hear other boys talk about his mom getting slammed, and knowing that it was probably true. That his home was broken was an understatement, and no secret to Patrick's friends or their parents. Why nobody had ever called child protective services was beyond him, but maybe par for the course. Aside from Sean, nobody seemed to care about Patrick.

Hell, after the house burned down and he had run away, the assholes hadn't even filed a report with the police. There was no story on the local news. No Amber Alert. No fliers. For all they knew he was dead, but to them a dead son was something to rejoice over. A dead son was one less mouth to feed.

Standing in front of the basement door, Patrick gripped the handle, turning the cold, brass knob. He swung the door open, wrinkling his nose as a musty stench from the depths of the basement rose up and assaulted his olfactory senses. The smell was strong enough to put his stomach in knots, easily overpowering the fresh scent of clean laundry. He took the steps slowly, his heart racing with each new step taking him closer to the one area of the house he had zero desire to be.

The old, wooden steps creaked. One of them had more give than Patrick thought acceptable, and for a moment his heart stopped when it cracked. Visions of falling through the stairs shot through his brain, and the image of being impaled on a shattered piece of wood stuck in his mind like a splinter stuck under a thumbnail.

Just get it over with. The quicker you get the clothes, the quicker you get the fuck out of the basement.

He took the last few steps two at a time, thinking of it in the same fashion as ripping off a band-aid. *Better to be done quickly than draw it out.*

At the bottom of the stairs, the basement split in two different directions. Straight ahead in the unfinished portion of the basement, the laundry room, water heater, and HVAC systems awaited. Off to the right, beyond a door that was locked at all times, lie a finished area of the basement that had once been used as a family room, but had long since ceased use for that purpose. Now that Patrick thought about it, in the almost decade that he had been friends with Sean, he had never known a time when that area of the basement had *not* been off limits.

Sean's father had caught the two of them trying to pick the lock years ago, and after the ass-whooping that Bobby had bestowed upon Sean for that particular transgression, they never made that attempt again. As far as either of them knew, Bobby used it as a man cave and home office. Why he was so adamant that the kids keep out of his area, Patrick couldn't say, but he knew that getting on Bobby's bad side was never a good idea.

Pat walked the path straight ahead stopping when he reached the dryer. Another streak of lightning illuminated the basement through the tiny windows, much too small to use as a point of egress were there to be a fire, or other such emergency requiring an immediate evacuation. The flash disappeared, leaving the basement darker than it had been. The hum of the HVAC system stopped.

The power was out, and now the generator had just shit the bed. Had lightning struck the house?

He snatched the basket off of the top of the machine and flung the door open so hard it smacked the wall and flew back, latching in place.

"What the fuck," he said, opening the dryer again, this time with care. He shoveled the warm clothes into the basket, not bothering to fold them. That could wait until he got out of this creepy ass basement.

Hellpp.

"What the fuck?" Patrick cried out, dropping the basket on the floor. There was no mistaking it this time—he had definitely heard a voice. The fucking place really was haunted. After all these years, and all the ball-busting they had done to their friends who had been too terrified of a basement to hang out, Patrick finally heard it himself. A small part of him felt bad for making fun of his friends, but only for a moment. He was too scared shitless at the moment to give much consideration to anything.

He sprinted to the steps, intending to haul ass up the stairs and out of the house when he heard the voice again, stopping him dead in his tracks.

Was it a ghost? There was no such thing, right? There had to be a rational explanation, because ghosts weren't real, and Patrick wasn't crazy. At least he didn't think he was crazy. There was no way he was hearing voices, right?

The voice called again, and Patrick responded, "Who's there?"

This time, the source of the voice remained silent. Maybe he *had* been hearing things. Between the power outage, the storm, and the local mystique that Patrick and friends had given the place as children, who could blame him for hearing strange sounds and attributing them to the supernatural.

Further internal debate sparked a morbid curiosity within Patrick's still maturing mind. The child in him told him to get the hell out. The teenager dancing with the prospect of adulthood told him he was being a pussy and needed to scope the basement out to prove to himself that there was no cause for alarm.

The testosterone coursing through his body won the war between his two selves. Patrick was no pussy.

Creeping through the dark like a thief in the night, Patrick strained the small muscles on either side of his head, perking his ears to better hear the sounds buried beneath the underlying house noises. He called again, hoping the voice would respond.

His attempt was not in vain: "Please, I'm in here."

It sounded to Patrick as if it came from the wall opposite the washer and dryer hookups, behind the furnace. Patrick pressed his ear to the wall. "Are you there?" he asked.

"Please, please let me out. I won't tell!"

Patrick couldn't believe it. There really was a voice coming from the basement. This was no hallucination; this was a living, breathing human. A person made of flesh and bone, same as he.

Patrick didn't know why someone would be behind the wall, but based on the location within the home, and Bobby Butler's reaction to finding him and Sean trying to break into his man cave, Patrick knew that Mr. Butler had a dark secret.

But how dark?

There was no telling, but Patrick had to assume the worst. He wasn't ignorant to the evils that men do. He'd been to the scared straight programs and watched the various prison reality shows on TLC and the like. And besides, was there any *good* reason to trap a human in a basement? Patrick thought if you were the one doing the trapping, maybe your fucked up mind could try to justify that, but no, there was no way to explain this one.

Knocking on the wall to test it, Patrick found the wall to be rock solid. He wouldn't be breaking in that way. He crept around the dark basement, trying to formulate a plan, but his eyes hadn't fully adjusted to the dark yet, making it difficult to see, nevermind rescue someone.

Patrick didn't give it much consideration, someone needed help, and with the power outage and his broken phone, he had no way to call for help. The responsibility to handle this situation rested solely upon his shoulders.

He hurried to the man cave door, knowing he would find it locked. The handle had no give, as expected. And although the door didn't seem to be reinforced, it was of solid construction and getting in would require a great deal of effort.

An idea sprouted inside Patrick's mind. It was so obvious. There was a four-foot tall toolbox next to the washer and dryer setup; there had to be something in there Patrick could use to force an entry into the room.

Patrick felt the blood pulsing through his veins, his blood pressure so high that he felt a throbbing sensation around his ears. He sifted through the toolbox, trying to find something that would do the trick. Luckily, he had been in the dark long enough that his eyes had adjusted to the lack of lighting in the basement since the power cut off. Neither locksmithing nor breaking and entering were his area of expertise, so he was unsure what exactly he would need to gain access to whatever lay beyond the door. After a few minutes of sifting through the drawers, he settled on a flathead screwdriver and a ball peen hammer.

Tools in hand, Patrick bounded back to the door, surveying it, trying to work out the best method of forced entry. With the hammer, he tried smashing the doorknob off, but that didn't do the trick. He succeeded in nothing more than mangling the knob, but the integrity of the locking mechanism remained.

Think!

The urgency of the situation caused him to overlook the obvious. He thought of an acronym a teacher had told him once, *K.I.S.S.*, *Keep it simple stupid.*

The hinges!

Dropping to his knees, Patrick tried to pry the pin from the hinge, but there wasn't enough space to get the tip in. With the flathead in one hand, and the hammer in the other, Patrick carefully lined the tip of the screwdriver up with the almost nonexistent space between the hinge and the pin. He tapped the base of the screwdriver with the hammer, slowly at first, but as the tip worked its way into the miniscule opening, prying it further apart, Patrick picked up the speed and intensity. As the speed and force with which Patrick worked steadily increased, so too did the noise generated by his actions. No longer could Patrick hear the raindrops splattering against the pavement as the storm raged outside. Patrick's singular focus on popping the hinges left him unaware of his surroundings, and he was no longer sure if the voice was still calling for help, but it mattered not, Patrick would not relent until he had broken through the door.

With one final smack of the hammer, the pin shot out of the hinge and fell to the floor in front of Patrick.

"Yes!" he said, picking the hinge up from its resting place. He turned the solid piece of metal about, giving an admiring glance to the object that had put up such resistance.

Patrick stood up, taking aim at the upper hinge. He placed the tip of the screwdriver against the small space…

Whack!

The leather pouch, filled with lead powder, bounced off the back of Patrick's head, the impact smashing his face into the door. Patrick lost consciousness even before hitting the door and dropped to the floor like a five-pound sack of shit.

A FIERCE THROBBING, PULSATING THROUGHOUT PATRICK'S skull greeted him upon his reentry into the land of the conscious. Vision blurry, he blinked repeatedly, trying to clear the cobwebs in his brain.

White lights, blinding in their luminescence, greeted Patrick upon the opening of his eyes. The intensity of the lights served only to increase the searing pain, leaving him prostrated and unable to compose himself enough to realize that he was strapped to a table. Minutes had passed before Patrick was aware enough of his surroundings to realize that there was something more than the pain in his head paralyzing him.

"What the fuck is this?" he said, finally aware of the leather straps binding his wrists, chest, and feet to the metal table.

Slowly, with his now returning strength, Patrick flexed his muscles, hoping to loosen the ties that bound him, and although he found they gave no purchase, he could sway his head. From the shoulders up, Patrick was unrestrained.

The dueling aromas of shit and buffalo sauce assaulted his nostrils.

Patrick turned his head to his left and something wet and sticky smacked him in the forehead, falling to the floor and leaving residue across his forehead.

Legs crossed, eating a bucket of chicken wings, Mr. Butler sat to Patrick's left. He smacked his chops, loudly chewing the wings and tossing them across the room at Patrick, where they plunked off of him and piled on the floor beneath his table.

"Boy, these are some delicious wings, Pat." Mr. Butler stood up and crossed the room in a flash, standing over Patrick. The rapid rise and fall of Mr. Butler's chest exposed the seething rage boiling underneath his calm exterior.

"Why are you doing this?" Patrick screamed.

Wiping the honey barbeque sauce from his lips, Mr. Butler grabbed Patrick's face, squeezing his cheeks. Flecks of chicken wings and spittle sprayed forth as he spoke. His voice was low and trembling, his sanity teeming on the verge of collapse. "Because you fucking made me do this,

Patrick. How's your Aunt Rita doing? Is she good? I'd imagine it might be tough to catch up with someone who DOESN'T FUCKING EXIST!"

Mr. Butler turned around and walked across the room.

Patrick took in his surroundings as his gaze followed his friend's psychotic father.

Sound proofing adorned the walls of the otherwise sterile environment of the room. One would be forgiven for mistaking the room for the OR of a hospital.

Or maybe that wouldn't be a mistake.

Mr. Butler disappeared through a doorway in the far corner of the room. Next to the doorway, in what could only be described as a large dog crate, a filthy teenage boy cowered in the fetal position. He was covered in filth. Blood and shit streaked across the boy and all over the crate.

The sad sight of the boy in the cage ended the mystery of the basement voice, and may well explain the cause of their childhood friends claiming to have heard ghosts in the house. With the soundproofing in this room, it was a wonder the boy's voice had carried through the basement. Patrick wondered how many other kids had been abducted by Mr. Butler. Piecing together all the times that Mr. Butler had acted strange regarding the basement, and the times Patrick's friends claimed to have heard ghosts, Patrick could only assume this had been going on for years. At least a decade, if he was correct about this.

Reemerging from the doorway, Mr. Butler pushed a table—identical to the one Patrick was bound to—into the room. "It wasn't supposed to be like this, Patrick. I have a system. I have an… order in which I go about things."

Patrick craned his neck, straining to see the body on the table.

It was hard to tell, but Patrick thought the body belonged to his friend, Haik.

Jesus, he's here because of me.

Mr. Butler crossed the room, stopping before a small table containing various gleaming instruments. The murderous tools twinkled in the bright light, a beauty which contradicted their deadly purpose. He selected a saw and crossed the room again, standing over the body.

Patrick's eyes shot open comically wide, although there was nothing funny about the situation. He watched as Mr. Butler set to work with the saw, pushing and pulling it back and forth. Wet, ripping noises turned to deeper, grinding sounds as the saw worked through flesh and meat before cutting into bone.

Patrick turned his head to look away, but vomited as he did so. The contents of his stomach sprayed forth and what didn't eject far enough slid back down his throat, threatening to choke him.

It would be a better death than whatever Mr. Butler had planned for him.

He closed his eyes, whispering the Lord's Prayer, despite not being a religious person.

"Funny how people find God when they are at the end of their rope, isn't it, Pat?" Mr. Butler placed something heavy on Patrick's chest. A wet warmth spread from the bottom of it and ran along either side of Patrick's bare chest.

"Open your eyes, Patrick."

Patrick, sobbing, did as he was told. He didn't want to further upset Mr. Butler. Even though he knew it wouldn't matter, a small part of Patrick's brain screamed for self-preservation, telling him that maybe there was a way out.

A severed head greeted Patrick as he opened his eyes.

He puked again.

"The delivery boy, Pat. YOU MADE ME KILL THE FUCKING DELIVERY BOY. YOU WEREN'T SUPPOSED TO BE HOME," Mr. Butler said, once more losing his cool.

Mr. Butler took a deep breath, held it, and exhaled. "I thought it was odd you wanted to go visit an aunt you've never once spoken of. Pat, you should have been with us on the trip. You weren't supposed to be here. You wouldn't be *here*," he said, gesturing at the table Patrick was strapped to. "But now," he continued, voice once more elevating, "now I have to take care of both you and your little friend."

Patrick cried. "Please, I won't tell anyone, just let me go." Tears rolled down his cheeks, and he choked once more, this time on sobs rather than the contents of his stomach.

"Do you think I'm a fucking idiot, Patrick? I can't let you go. Even if I trusted you, which I don't, you've caused me too much trouble. You can disappear easy enough, a troubled kid whose parents didn't give a fuck enough about him to leave an address or a phone number when they disappeared to wherever the hell they went. I've searched for them, and they're gone. They don't want to be found. *You* won't be found. This *fucking* delivery boy though. What are the odds that he walked around the side of the house, and just happened to see you and I when I caught you at the door?" Mr. Butler shook his head. "Pretty fucking good, I guess, because I caught the little son-of-a-bitch spying on us through the window. Thank god this porker couldn't move to save his life."

Patrick zoned out. He couldn't take Mr. Butler's rant any longer, he was going to die here in this basement. Nobody would care. He had no family to speak of, and the only friend who'd miss him lived with the monster poised to snuff out the flame of his life before it ever had time to burn bright.

There was no hope.

No chance of escape.

Resigned to his fate, Patrick closed his eyes. "Just do it," he said. "Put me out of my misery."

"Put you out of your misery? No, I won't be doing that. I promise you're going to suffer long and hard for what you've done. No quick end for you, son. But there will be *plenty* of misery."

Mr. Butler grabbed a nasty-looking instrument and set to work with the precision of a surgeon and the fury of a sociopath who knew his world was in danger of collapsing, burying him under the weight of his sins. The two additional bodies in his basement would be too much for him to keep under wraps, but bloodlust had taken over and he would finish the task, no matter what happened when it was over.

Using a pair of needle-nose pliers, Mr. Butler set about Patrick's thumb, pulling the nail up, slowly. It lifted easily enough at first until the skin and tissue holding the nail in place reached their limit of elasticity. He increased the pressure, slowly separating it from the meat of the finger. Blood flowed from the wound, and Patrick writhed in pain, screaming, trying to escape the torture.

The leather straps killed any form of resistance.

After removing the nails from Patrick's hands and feet, Mr. Butler turned his attention to Patrick's waist. Now lost in his work, and excited to continue, he absentmindedly adjusted the bulge in his pants before grabbing Patrick's flaccid cock.

Mr. Butler stared in wonder at Patrick's meat, impressive even when limp. "Wow, quite the shame that you'll never be using this again. I almost feel bad for the women you'll never get to fuck."

Patrick said nothing, he had passed out by the time Mr. Butler had begun work on his toes.

Disappointed in the lack of response from Patrick, Mr. Butler got back to work. He selected a scalpel from his tools of terror and ran the blade across Patrick's testicles. The sack split open and blood flowed around Patrick's thighs, pooling on the table beneath his ass cheeks.

Running the blade along the length of Patrick's shaft, Mr. Butler used his free hand to stroke the not so impressive length of his own. The excitement of a fresh plaything became too much for him to handle, despite the imminent threat of discovery the two unplanned kills brought about, and before he could guide Patrick down the path toward whatever lay beyond the mortal realm, he first had to usher himself across the threshold of ecstasy.

With the finish line mere strokes away, Mr. Butler gripped himself tighter and stroked with a relentless pace. The veins in his neck bulged as his face flushed and a pathetically small load spurt forth from his throbbing micro penis.

With the sweet release of orgasm achieved, Mr. Butler picked up where he left off, working quickly to bring a different sweet release to Patrick.

But not *too* quickly.

Mr. Butler may be a sociopath, but he kept his promise to Patrick, making sure that he kept his son's friend alive long enough to suffer for all the trouble he caused him.

After all, a man was only as good as his word, and Mr. Butler always kept his.

Open The Window, Tommy

Halloween 2012 was the last Halloween of my childhood. Hell, it was the last time I ever went out after dark, even now in my twenties. There are… things out there, things unseen in the daytime. Most people will tell you they don't exist. That's what they told me. They told me I was mistaken, that the dark, and the fear played tricks on my mind. But I know what I saw, and I know when the sun goes down, the scared ones are the smart ones, because from dusk 'til dawn, nobody is safe.

———

Trick or treating, I had no desire for such a childish thing. At 13, I was much too old to be seen in a costume begging for candy; I had better things to do. But, as parents are wont to do, our mother had taken the wind out of my sails and informed me that if I had any intent on going to the Halloween party that evening, I would first be taking Ralphie out for candy.

I couldn't believe the audacity of that woman. So

against the idea of trick or treating was I, that I had almost said *fuck it* and skipped the party. If I were to be seen trick or treating with my younger brother, my high school career was finished before it ever had a chance to truly begin. But, as a horny freshman, I wanted to see what outfits the senior girls were going to wear to the party, and what teenage boy wouldn't take that risk?

After rushing Ralphie through a route that I had picked out—through the richest neighborhood, of course—we hopped on our bikes and hauled ass like our lives depended on it. As it so happened, they would.

We pedaled down Budlong Road, only a few miles from our house. A few miles until I was free from Ralphie and ready to mingle with some hotties. Of course, when I say *mingle* I mean awkwardly stare and not dare to approach them. The pecking order of high school class rank was real, and I was well aware freshmen were the bottom rung of the ladder.

Along the right side of the road was a stretch of woods. They weren't especially deep in this area, but it was densely populated, meaning that although you could easily cut through the woods and be on the other side in a few minutes, you couldn't see a damn thing beyond the tree line.

We sped along the road, I was eager to get home and to the party, Ralphie was afraid of what lie beyond the woods.

Glennwood Cemetery. Everyone knew it was haunted. Well, that was the local legend, anyway. But really, what cemetery *wasn't* haunted. The damn places were stuffed to the brim with dead bodies.

A blood-curdling scream pierced the trees, startling me, and sending me flying over my handlebars into the ditch at the foot of the tree line.

Ralphie skidded to a halt, dismounted his bike, and ran to where I sat, brushing the leaves and dirt off of my pants. Though physically unharmed, my pride had taken a hit.

"Tommy, are you ok?" he said.

"Yeah, I'm good."

The hair on my neck stood at attention and goose pimples sprouted along my arms. A chill ran the length of my spine, despite the unseasonably warm weather and the zip-up hoodie I wore.

"What do you think that was?" Ralphie asked.

"A scream, dumbass."

This shut Ralphie up.

"It sounded like someone in the cemetery. Glennwood is just behind these trees. It's not even a five-minute walk through the woods from here," I said.

"Why would someone be in the cemetery at night?"

I could think of a few reasons. Some good, some not so good. We should have gotten on our bikes and continued home. After all, I was a young teen carting around my kid brother; I would be no use to anyone, but sometimes we do stupid shit without really considering the consequences. For most people, those bad choices end up as nothing more than a story to tell, but sometimes, we aren't so lucky. Ralphie and I, we weren't so lucky.

"Let's find out," I said, walking into the tree line. There was no need to look back to make sure Ralphie followed me. I knew my brother; he was petrified in the dark. He would have followed me to the depths of hell if it meant he wouldn't be alone at night.

Sure enough, I heard him cry out, "Wait up, don't leave me!"

I crept through the woods, Ralphie at my heels. A branch snapped behind me. I turned and gave him a death stare while placing my finger to my lips. *Quiet*, I mouthed.

He took the hint.

Staying close behind, he managed to not make another peep. I was shocked, really. Though shallow, the pathless woods could be treacherous, especially at night. Densely packed trees, fallen detritus, and exposed tree roots made covertness nigh impossible. The little shit was finally doing something right. I was proud.

The moon hung in the sky, full, all its luminous glory exposing the things that go bump in the night. But in the woods between Budlong road and Glenwood Cemetery, even the lunar illumination could not penetrate the thick trees. It made me glad the woods were not deep, otherwise we may never find the other side.

The edge of the tree line awaited us less than twenty yards from where we stood. I could hear soft whimpering ahead, coming from the graveyard. The sound, louder now, was a mixture of pain and ecstasy. In my teenage mind, it sounded not unlike the late night sounds coming from the bedroom of two parents who aren't sure if the children are asleep, and so they must keep the noise down.

Ralphie and I pressed on until we reached the edge of the trees. We stood there for a moment, scanning the graveyard for any sign of life.

Smacking and slurping sounds emanated from the space between two rows of graves, and for a moment, I thought I may have been right about what those sounds meant.

Now that we were out of the woods the moon's illumination left the graveyard exposed for all eyes to see, and though my eyes saw clearly, it took my brain much longer to compute the abomination that lay ahead.

"What is it?" Ralphie said.

My arm shot out, my hand clamping his mouth shut.

Ahead, the thing looked up from its feast. Blood

smeared its lips, a crimson mask from the nose down. In its horrid embrace, a brunette haired woman. She was young, early twenties. Her pirate shirt ripped open, rivers of blood ran in between the twin peaks of her chest. I remember being slightly turned on at the sight. You can't blame me, I was 13, and testosterone ran amok in my body. At that age the *word* breast was liable to bring on a four-hour erection.

Despite the ragged wound at her neck, she moaned as if in pleasure, not pain. From the way her hand slowly worked below her belt, it was likely both of those things.

The monstrosity snarled and snapped its prey's neck, letting her hit the ground as it rose to its full height.

Standing tall, it reached well over six feet. I locked eyes with it and found myself unable to move; I was in the creature's thrall.

Ralphie shrieked, that ear piercing shriek that only young children can seem to muster, snapping me into action. I grabbed my brother by the wrist, turned, and ran like someone had lit a fire underneath my ass.

We crashed through the woods, stumbling over tree roots. I was in the lead, with Ralphie somehow keeping pace. Extended in front of me, the palm of my hand acted as a shield for low hanging branches that would have easily put an eye out. Even still, by the time we reached the road I looked as if I had gone twelve full rounds with Manny Pacquiao.

We grabbed our bikes from the ditch, hopped on, and pedaled as fast as our bikes would take us.

It wasn't fast enough.

From the tree line, I heard a rustling. The thing was chasing us now. We had interrupted its indulgence, and now it had marked us for death.

I stood on my pedals and, leaning forward with my

teeth clenched, I pumped my legs like a boy possessed. "Faster, Ralphie!" I shrieked.

I heard a snarl and a thud behind me, followed by the unmistakable sound of Ralphie's blood-curdling scream. I pissed my pants in fear. Fear for my life. Fear for Ralphie's, too.

I jammed the pedals on my Dyno bike, slamming the brakes and doing a 180.

On its hands and knees, the bloodthirsty fiend drew sustenance from Ralphie.

I dropped the bike to the ground, I had to do something quick. In need of a weapon. A quick scan of the area revealed not much of use. I grabbed the largest branch I could come up with on short notice and wielded it like a club. I would bludgeon the son of a bitch and rescue my brother. "Let him go!"

Its head snapped up, whipping its long black hair backwards and out of its face. The essence of my brother's life dripped from its two long fangs. Large red eyes pierced me to my very core, stopping me in my tracks once again. Something about its gaze, the way it looked into your very soul, it made you a prisoner in your own body, powerless to act.

I dropped the stick. The creature, sensing no threat, returned its attention to Ralphie.

No longer holding my gaze, I eventually snapped out of my trance, but I was too terrified to act. I got on my bike and pedaled away as fast as possible, telling myself Mom would know what to do. I knew it was bullshit; I was a coward, but I was also a kid and self-preservation won the internal battle.

I kept pedaling, long after the slurping sounds ceased. After the sobbing died, and Ralphie along with them.

———

RALPHIE'S body, or whatever was left of it, was never recovered. Again and again, I told my parents the truth of what happened that evening. She thought I was losing my mind. The police didn't believe me, either. Why would they? What sane adult would believe that a creature of the night feasted upon my brother? The remains of the young woman were nowhere to be found, either. Eventually, detectives determined that Ralphie had been the final victim of a child predator in the area. The creature I described to them matched the description of a man who had been spotted on multiple occasions near other "missing" children. It wasn't an exact match, of course, but the thing I saw was close enough to nail the man with multiple charges.

The man they arrested for the death of Ralphie admitted to the kidnapping, torture, molestation, and eventual death of more than fifteen children in Rhode Island over a ten year period. Ralphie was the only one that he vehemently denied having anything to do with.

That man rotted in jail, and although he deserved to, I know the truth. That man was not responsible for the disappearance of Ralphie. The man responsible was no man, but a creature. One who didn't prey only on children. Men, women, children—all were potential meals to that beast.

From that evening forward, I did my best to avoid being out after dark. As I said earlier, there are things in the dark that shouldn't exist.

I grew up sooner than any teenager should.

But Ralphie?

Ralphie never grew up.

Every Halloween Ralphie shows up at my window.

Even now, after all this time. He never forgot about me, even though I abandoned him. He tells me it's water under the bridge, that he forgives me. Ralphie tells me he has a gift for me: eternal life.

If only I open the window.

Tonight is the tenth anniversary of Ralphie's death, and as much as I love my brother, and regret abandoning him, I never opened the window. Not even on the days when my guilt was at its worst.

I think tonight I'll open my window, though.

I miss my brother.

The Newlyweds

Floating along the dying waves of inebriation, Tony drifted back onto the shores of consciousness, his body rebelling against the excessive amount of alcohol he had consumed the night prior. "You only get married once!" he'd told everyone as he pounded drink after drink. Fun fact: Mary was his third wife and the humor of that joke was lost on their guests.

What Tony didn't find funny was waking to a skull-splitting hangover made worse by the sun's rays shining through the curtains in their hotel suite. The hotel charged enough money they could certainly afford functional curtains, not these fancy but useless pieces of shit.

Tony sat up too quickly, and a fit of dry-heaving stopped him in place. He hacked up nothing but bloody sputum and thin, yellow streaks of stomach bile. When the bout of nausea passed, he attempted to get up again, this time much slower. He stretched, careful to make no sudden movements, lest he puke again. Taking in a deep breath, the rancid scent of old vomit and alcohol hit him like a liver punch from Mike Tyson.

"Jesus Christ," he said, his voice hoarse from all of the dry heaving and vomiting.

Tony looked at the California king bed, now empty, aside from the dried, crusty bodily fluids desecrating the hotel linens, and a pair of red, crotchless, lace panties.

The panties did not belong to Mary.

Where is that fucking bitch?

Mary was hardly a bitch. Tony knew that, but he wasn't someone that people considered a *good man*, so to him, most women were bitches, including his wife. The Maid of Honor's discarded undergarments on his bed the morning after his wedding was a fine example of his character.

A brief tour of the suite led Tony to discover Mary passed out on the sleeper sofa in the living area. Dressed in her loungewear, she clearly hadn't endured the rough night Tony did.

He wasn't sure at what point Mary had left the bedroom, or if she had ever made it to bed, although he made an educated guess and surmised that she had probably not even entered the suite until Tony finished rearranging her best friend's guts.

And that summed up Mary in a nutshell. The timid, soft spoken woman who was too meek to stand up for herself on her wedding night while her husband bent her maid of honor over their bed. In a way, Tony thought that was very considerate of her, because god damn was the maid of honor the single best piece of ass he'd ever gotten. Not that he remembered much of the sex, but he knew what she looked like, and he wanted to believe the sex had been that good.

Tony stood over his bride. "Mary, get your ass up."

Mary stirred, rubbing the sleep from her eyes.

For a moment, Tony thought he saw a flash of intensity

in those deep blue eyes, but it was gone in an instant, replaced with the demure nature Mary was known for.

She sat up, scrambling into the corner of the couch, burying herself in it.

That was another thing that pissed Tony off about her. She had this pathetic habit of making herself as tiny as possible, like a wounded rabbit playing dead. Not that she *shouldn't* be afraid of him—just ask wife number two, God rest her soul—but Tony had barely laid a hand on her in their time together, and while he liked his women to know their place, it seemed to him that Mary knew hers a bit prematurely. Like she was acting how she *thought* Tony wanted her to act, and not how Tony had *trained* her to act.

And therein lied part of the problem. Mary's bullshit was costing Tony the opportunity to train her, a task he deeply enjoyed. And although her lack of spunk cost him the joy of putting her in her place, she was a necessary evil.

After the ex-wife disappeared, the cops had pinned Tony as the prime suspect—excellent detective work, all things considered—but Tony had been doing this far too long to be caught by the likes of the local PD, and had covered his tracks expertly, managing to avoid formal charges.

Scrutiny from the law didn't end there, however, and Tony knew that he had to construct a life that would hold up under a microscope.

That's where shy little Mary came in.

Mary, the quiet high-school librarian. While he preferred a woman with a spine so he could break her down bit by bit, he supposed Mary was actually a good fit. Her demeanor was not likely to test his limits, thus pushing him to dispose of her. Going hands on with the women he dated was commonplace, and breaking a woman to the point where he controlled her and had zero fears of retaliation or outside involvement was damn near an orgasmic experience to him. He tried his best to refrain from letting the women close to him see him for who he *really* was. One didn't last as long as Tony did when the women closest to him had a habit of vanishing. But sometimes when a bitch acted up, as the ex had, that bitch needed to disappear with the rest of them.

"You know, we never consummated our marriage, Love," Tony said, playing with his cock, which was girthy even at half-mast.

Mary flashed a smile. "I know, honey. You just drank so much last night and I didn't think you wanted to be bothered."

She knows. She is so weak that she knows I stuffed her whore of a friend and filled that bitch up with all the cock she could handle, and she won't even confront me about it! Maybe she really is the one. It will be nothing to keep this bitch in check, and she's too much of a doormat to ever ask questions.

The realization that he had indeed chosen the right woman to prop up his public facing life left Tony aroused. The prospect of continuing his…extracurricular activities was indeed a sexual feeling for him. Needing relief for the throbbing between his legs, he grabbed the back of her head, forcing it toward his massive prick.

Although Mary's meek nature went up Tony's ass, he had no complaints about her sex game. A wise man once said he wanted a lady in the streets but a freak in the bed, and god damn if Mary wasn't a freak. She fucked like a prostitute and sucked cock like her life depended on it.

Even now, hungover, Tony was approaching climax like it was the first time a woman played his skin flute. Mary worked the shaft like a magician, twisting her wrist while bobbing up and down, making his Italian sausage disappear in the back of her throat. An impressive trick indeed.

Tony tried to hold back his orgasm, but Mary must have sensed the impending cum shot. She gripped tighter and deepthroated his cock. With his balls tight against her chin and head deep in her throat, Tony came. His meat pulsated, sending thick spurts of warm semen straight down her gullet. No need to swallow, not even a drop touched her tongue.

"That's good, baby," Tony said, gripping her chin with his thumb and index finger. "Now get your ass up. We need to wash up and get to the airport before we miss our flight."

———

AFTER HOURS OF NAVIGATING AIRPORT SECURITY, TONY and Mary took their seats. Still recovering from excessive alcohol consumption, exhaustion plagued him, leaving Tony downtrodden and miserable. His head pounded something fierce and his stomach threatened to expel the meager bits of food and coffee he managed to keep down. Mary appeared to be in good spirits, a fact that went up Tony's ass. Her lack of drinking meant that she would not spend the day battling her own body the way Tony would. Misery loves company, and Tony hates feeling lonely.

That goodie fucking two-shoes, he thought, breathing in deeply, concentrating on the rise and fall of his chest, trying to keep the beast locked inside of him. It was difficult. There were times when he just wanted to let it free, consequences be damned. He knew he needed to ease up on the heavy drinking, and although the marriage was nothing more than a sham to him, he intended on enjoying the honeymoon. He had paid for it, after all, and it was tough to enjoy a vacation when you spent most of it praying to the porcelain God, your face inches from shit streaks and piss stains.

The pressure of building a false life to cover his tracks wore on him, at times cracking the exterior facade, but at least he realized it, and a new wife put him on the road to fixing the problem.

Sitting on the uncomfortable airplane seat, reflecting on the path he traveled, and what led him to this point, he kept coming back to Mary and the fact that despite being the perfect cover, *something* about her bugged him, and he couldn't place his finger on *what*. He should be thrilled to find a woman like her, but the nagging feeling wouldn't go away. It was like a worm, wriggling in his brain.

It wasn't just the fact that he was hungover and she wasn't. That pissed him off, sure, but that was his problem and had nothing to do with the feeling he got from her lately.

Her choice of destination for the honeymoon had been odd, and sitting here on the plane, he still could not make heads or tails of it. Mary wasn't an outdoor person, and she especially hated being around large groups of people. A few months ago he tried to surprise her with a trip to the beach and she had freaked out. At first, he thought it was the thong bikini he'd tossed at her, but after getting her to calm down, he'd learned it had nothing to do with the bikini—she'd be happy to show off that perfectly shaped peach—just not in front of a packed beach of perverts who'd no doubt take a mental snapshot for the spank bank.

Leave it to Tony, he sure knew how to pick the fucking winners, alright. He caught himself getting mad again, taking a deep breath. Forcing himself to think positively, he focused on the fact that Mary had changed her mind about crowds and beach-going perverts. Going out of her comfort zone to book a Caribbean cruise vacation, risking her mental health to make him happy. She really was a good woman, and if Tony wasn't such a piece of shit, he might actually treat her the way a woman deserved to be treated.

Mary looked at Tony and smiled. Tony smiled back, not out of love, but because in his sick mind, he found the timing of her smile funny. He reached for her hand, letting her have the moment. They both fell asleep and remained that way for the duration of the flight to Florida.

———

THE FLIGHT HAD BEEN LONG, AND UNUSUALLY TURBULENT. Tony hardly slept a wink and ended up blowing chunks again. They left the baggage claim, clumsily dragging their luggage with them. Tony hadn't bothered reserving a rental car ahead of time and when they showed up at the counter, all of the companies that operated out of the airport parking garage were out of vehicles. It seemed like bullshit to Tony. He didn't understand how they could have *nothing*, but since the pandemic had struck things had changed in every industry, and while people were eager to get back in the groove of things, many businesses had not caught up yet and things were far from normal.

The two newlyweds walked into the humid Florida night and hailed an Uber. The driver must have been circling the airport, waiting for a client like a vulture circling carrion in the desert because it had only taken a few short minutes for him to arrive almost as if he had materialized out of thin air.

The driver exited the vehicle and made a show of grabbing their bags for them, doing his best to show them he would go the extra mile for their convenience—and a tip, of course.

After loading the couple's bags in the trunk, the driver made his way to the passenger side of the blacked out SUV, opening the door for them, waving them into the vehicle with an exaggerated gesture of the hand.

Chivalry be damned, Tony slid into the backseat. He didn't give two fucks about letting Mary get in first, he was still tired and needed to sit in the air conditioned vehicle before he lost his fucking mind. He leaned against the driver side window, watching his wife chat up the driver.

Is she flirting with him?

Impossible. Mary wasn't the type. If the Uber driver had been the opposite sex, and had either a fat ass or nice tits, Tony would be out there flirting for sure, but not *his* Mary. She wouldn't.

Would she?

Mary laughed, playfully slapping the driver's shoulder before climbing into the vehicle and buckling up.

"What the fuck was that, Mary?" Tony asked.

"What was what?"

"Really? You don't know? You practically threw your pussy at him. Want me to switch spots with him so you can suck his cock before we get on the boat?"

Anger flashed across Mary's usually soft face. "First off, Tony, don't you ever talk to me like that again. I won't have it. I'm not some cheap slut.". She bit her lip, paused and took a deep breath. The spark of emotion that had crossed her face was gone, and she spoke in a measured tone. "Tony, he told me a joke. That's all. I thought it was funny, I'm sorry. I understand why you thought it looked like that. I'm sorry. I didn't mean anything by it."

That was the first time in their relationship that Tony had seen Mary display any kind of anger, or even a harsh tone. It didn't take long for Mary to revert back to her timid self, but something about what just happened didn't sit right with him, and it added to that nagging feeling he kept getting.

Tony decided to let it go, put it in his back pocket. Something to store for future reference. But only because they were on their honeymoon, and she had never pulled any shit like that before. If she slipped up again though, got a little lip, well, then he couldn't be responsible for teaching her a little respect.

Mary smiled at Tony, and Tony smiled back. Tony wasn't so sure that his smile was the only fake one anymore.

———

MARY GREW WEARY OF TONY'S BULLSHIT. THE MAN WAS infuriating, a lunatic, and a grade-A piece of shit. But he was her husband, and she held his hand the duration of the ride to the Marriott, Orlando, even though she harbored little desire for romance. The gesture was insincere, nothing more than allowing a narcissist to feel like he'd taken her subservience. She didn't know how much longer she could keep this up, but she needed to be sure Tony was who she thought he was. She had rules. They could be broken, sure, but it was more fun when there was…a hunter involved.

Mary hoped that the shy, timid, nice girl act would bring out the worst in him. That it would sicken him to the point of exposing himself. The real Tony. It was in his nature, but for some reason Tony simply would not be who she thought he was. But she couldn't be wrong. She'd done her research. Her due diligence. Mary was *never* wrong.

Sure, he was loud. He bossed her around, and he had even put hands on her. But that wasn't enough. Plenty of men put their hands on a woman, but never took it further.

Why wasn't Tony willing to take the next step? She had spent months cowering, groveling, making herself a *victim*. But instead of killing her, he *popped the question*. What the hell had she done wrong?

With her original tactic not working, not bringing out the killer in him, Mary decided to switch gears. If she couldn't get him to strike by acting like a doormat, she would provoke him. Poke the bear, so to speak. The driver had been a spur of the moment thing, but it got Tony's attention.

It was easy enough; she hadn't even tried. She had simply made no effort to hide the fact that she lusted after their driver. He smelled so good that when he reached in front of her to open the door, it had sent a tremble through her sex, and so she had flirted with him. Nothing crazy, but she wished Tony *had* switched places with the driver, instead of using that rhetorical question as a dagger in an argument.

The SUV pulled up to the hotel and the driver let them out. He attempted to take their bags out of the trunk, but Tony stopped him. Mary could practically see the steam coming from Tony's head, and from the look on his face, she half expected him to knock the driver out right there in the hotel drop off.

They walked their bags to the front desk and checked into the hotel. The concierge asked them if they wanted a cart, but Tony had said no. She didn't blame him. Those carts were awkward, and navigating the hallways was a hassle when utilizing them.

They took the elevator, and when they arrived at the door Tony swiped the keycard and walked into the room. Mary couldn't believe it. This piece of shit couldn't even be bothered to scoop his wife up and bring her to bed.

She followed Tony into the room, letting the door slam

shut behind her before standing next to him on the side of the bed.

Tony wasted no time, pushing Mary onto the bed and flipping her around, yanking her pants down so her ass was exposed, only covered by a barely there pair of blue lace booty shorts.

"What are you doing?" she asked, feigning surprise.

"You," he said.

Mary didn't want to let Tony touch her, but she was horny. The driver was handsome, and smelled delicious. Again she regretted not sucking his cock. Hell, if she had done it, that might have pushed Tony over the edge.

Tony struggled to pull the underwear to the side enough to fit his cock in. Mary sighed and pulled them down. For a guy who thought he was a stud, he had trouble keeping things hot. He was like a teenage boy who thought he knew what he was doing. A big cock, but practically good for nothing.

Spitting on his hand, he greased his cock with the saliva soaked palm of one hand, and grabbed her ponytail with the other.

She chuckled under her breath. No need for the spit tonight. Tony didn't do it for her, but she was still wet from earlier. As Tony shoved his massive cock inside of her, she quivered, imagining it was the driver.

He pounded away, lasting a full forty-five seconds before telling Mary he was going to "fill her little pussy up."

Mary hadn't stopped thinking about the driver, and went to town on her clit while Tony got himself off. She couldn't believe a guy with a cock that big could be so bad at sex, but here she was, on the cusp of faking another orgasm because her husband had the stamina of a two pump chump.

Mary couldn't wait to be done with Tony; he was the worst yet. At least the others had been good at sex. What a waste of cock he was.

As Tony shot his seed into her, Mary brought herself to climax, thankful that she would fall asleep satisfied for once.

Tony rolled over, pulling the comforter off of her, hogging them to himself. He was asleep within moments.

———

THE FIRST DAY AND A HALF ABOARD THE CRUISE HAD PASSED uneventfully. They attended a couple of the shows that played in the auditorium, tried out a few of the boat's restaurants, and drank copious amounts of alcohol. Par for the course. Mary surprised Tony yet again, upping her alcohol consumption the past few days. Up until the cruise she hadn't been a drinker, and now that Tony thought about it, he couldn't really recall a time where she had been drunk. Buzzed? Tony couldn't say. Maybe she was more of a goodie two shoes than Tony had thought. He had to hand it to her, the woman had kept up with him drink for drink and looked none the worse for wear. She wasn't human; she was a machine.

Tony had said as much to her after the first night of pounding drinks, and Mary had laughed it off. "My metabolism is crazy," she said.

What the hell does that even mean? He knew what she meant, but was she serious? That was the real question. Not that it mattered, in the grand scheme of things. Having a wife that could drink you under the table didn't really count for anything. If she took this act home and started making him seem like a bitch, well that was a different story. But for now, he would let sleeping dogs lie.

Still, he was a bit embarrassed, tripping over himself, hardly able to stand, while his wife—who was half his size—drank like a fish and still managed to nurse him during his drunken stupor.

Around noon, Tony woke up, his head pounding something fierce. They had really tied one on again last night. Mary had fed him drinks all night long, and seemed to have another drink waiting for him before he'd even finished the one in front of him.

He sat up, slowly. He rubbed his aching shoulder, and as he touched the spot in question, a fiery, piercing pain shot through the area.

Hissing, he pulled his hand away, the pain was too much, his head swimming. He looked down at his hand, noticing it was slick. Warm and sticky. "What the fuck?" he said. Was that blood? He couldn't tell, the shades aboard the cruise ship working much better than the pieces of shit that had adorned the windows of the hotel room.

Tony rose from the bed, making his way gingerly across the room. He opened the shades, letting the sunlight in despite what it would do to his already pounding skull.

With the blackout shades drawn open, Tony gazed at the bedside mirror, inspecting the problem area.

He squinted in the mirror, shocked at the discovery. An open wound sat in the hollow of his shoulder, multiple lacerations grouped together in a small oval. Tony grabbed the bedsheets, giving them a once over. He found the linens to be covered in crimson stains. It looked as if a good amount of blood had saturated them. The bleeding had definitely slowed since… whatever the hell he had done last night while he was drunk.

"Mary? Mary, what the hell did I do last night?" he called.

Mary didn't respond, and Tony wondered where she

had gotten off too. He thought she was in the bathroom, but if she was, she was ignoring him, and that wasn't like her. Then again, it wasn't like her to disappear, either. Had they gotten into a fight last night? Tony couldn't recall an argument, although he had blacked out, so it was entirely possible things had gotten out of hand.

Jesus Christ, If I did something to her, it could blow my cover.

Tony needed to find Mary. With no recollection of the prior night, he would need her to fill in the gaps. Hopefully he hadn't laid a finger on her. That would complicate things.

As Tony stood in front of the dresser, Mary entered the room. She moved silently, creeping like a thief in the night. She moved as if she had no idea Tony was watching her. He couldn't believe it. Was she really that stupid?

"Where the fuck were you?" he yelled.

Mary jumped, and the door slammed shut behind her. "Oh, Tony, you're awake," she said, her back leaning against the door. Her hair was disheveled and her makeup a mess. She still wore the dress she wore to dinner the night before.

"I sure am. Looks like you've been up for a while, too. You want to tell me where you've been? And why the fuck you're sneaking around like a burglar?"

"I was at the infirmary. I tweaked my back carrying you to bed last night. I couldn't even get undressed. It hurt so bad I couldn't reach the zipper between my shoulders. I tried sleeping it off, but when I woke up this morning my back was shot and I almost couldn't get out of bed. The doctor gave me some pain relievers and muscle relaxers. I figured you were still sleeping it off so I tried not to make too much noise."

Tony didn't know how to take that one. Something about it seemed... off, but at the same time, he couldn't disprove what she was telling him, nor did he have a grasp on what he thought she might be attempting to do. He simply knew that she wasn't telling the truth. Call it a gut feeling.

Tony crossed the room, looked Mary up and down. He sniffed her like an animal. He wanted to intimidate her, make her feel uncomfortable. Maybe she would fess up to whatever she had done. Tony didn't know, but he thought putting the fear of God in her might get her to sing like a canary. But what if he was wrong? Mary had never really done anything to give Tony cause for concern.

Except for that fucking attitude the other night, he thought. His mind kept circling back to the way she had acted the last few days. The attitude, the flirtation with the Uber driver, and more recently, her inhuman adjustment to massive alcohol intake.

There was something about Mary…

"Any idea what the hell happened to my shoulder?" he said.

There was a split second, almost undetectable, but Tony caught it, where Mary's face changed upon hearing the question. It was as if she wanted to say something but caught herself. "You broke a glass."

"I broke a glass? Where? How the hell did I cut my shoulder?"

"I don't know. I wasn't there. I was in the bathroom. I came out and you were bleeding."

That didn't pass the sniff test and now he *knew* Mary was holding something back. What that was, he wasn't sure, but he was going to find out. He'd let her have her fake little victory now, let her feel like she pulled a fast one. But Mary was going to learn a lesson, that was for God damn sure.

"Well, now that you got your shit taken care of at

medical, why don't you get your ass over here and take care of this shoulder for me."

"I can't, Tony. You know how I feel about blood. I can't do it."

Tony was pissed. Absolutely fuming. He needed to get out of this room before Mary had an unfortunate accident. One there was no coming back from. The first investigation had been a close call and he narrowly avoided criminal charges. He didn't like the over-under on dodging lightning twice.

Throwing on soiled jeans and a crumpled t-shirt he picked up off of the bedroom floor, Tony shouldered his way past Mary, slamming the door closed on his way out.

———

MARY CROSSED THE ROOM AND SAT ON THE BED, SMILING AT the door. The seeds were planted. Tony would make a move soon. She had pushed his buttons and set the wheels in motion. He was a hothead, she knew that. And she knew it wouldn't take long for him to come back ready to teach her a lesson.

Mary was still horny from the night prior, and with nothing to do but wait for Tony to make a move, Mary lay back on the bed and masturbated. Whatever plan he concocted, she thought that the brain between his legs wouldn't be able to resist one last fuck. So she would lie in wait, playing with herself while replaying her escapades from the night prior. In her mind's eye, the three studs she met at the bar ran another train on her.

Drugging him was a great idea, she thought. She had been on the fence about it, initially, but if she hadn't she wouldn't have been in the position to take three cocks, nor would she be in the position now to finish Tony.

As she approached climax, Mary's mind shuffled through images of last night's sexcapades, Tony's lacerated shoulder, and her impending confrontation with the man the media knew as "The Cranston Crippler."

———

"That fucking bitch. I knew there was something up," he said. Tony couldn't fathom why she would lie, especially not one with more holes in it than Swiss cheese. Was she afraid of him? That had to be it. Because she couldn't be so stupid as to think he would let that one slide. She had to know he'd uncover the truth, right? The wound was gnarly. It was a safe bet that his first stop would be medical to get it looked at, and all he had to do was ask if she'd been in there a few short minutes ago.

Stewing in his anger and reflecting on their brief conversation, Tony should have pushed the issue with it further. Of course she hadn't been in the infirmary getting her back looked at. She didn't look like she was in pain. She looked like she'd finished getting her brains fucked out, but Tony was fighting a hangover and the possibility that he was on a honeymoon with a whore hadn't occurred to him until moments ago.

He was pissed, but part of him—the part between his thighs—was a bit turned on, not because he was a Cuck, but because if his wife *was* a whore, there might be some fun times on the horizon.

The problem was Mary wasn't going to live to see another day.

———

Tony swiped the keycard and the light flashed green. A *snickt* noise sounded as the locking mechanism disengaged. He flung the door open and it bounced off the doorstop before swinging back. He managed to catch the door before it whacked him in the face, narrowly avoiding a shattered nose.

Mary wasn't going to be so lucky.

Storming through the door, Tony shouted "Mary, get the fuck…" he stopped short, the words catching in his throat.

Mary lay on the bed, propped on her elbows with her legs spread wide. Most of her body weight was supported with her left arm, the right was furiously pumping a large, purple dildo in and out of her pussy. She still wore last night's dress, but it was hiked up around her waist and one strap had slid down her shoulder, exposing a portion of her breast. Ecstasy painted her white face with splotches of red as the dildo stretched her pussy, wet slapping sounds accompanied drops of vaginal secretions as the fake balls on the dildo stopped the rubber organ from disappearing.

Tony had never seen his wife in such a vulnerable position. Sure, he'd had his way with her plenty of times, and she was no prude, that's for sure, but never had he witnessed her going to town on herself with such reckless abandon. The sight turned him on, and while he had a bone to pick with her, Tony thought maybe he had a bone to stick *in* her first. From six to midnight in an instant, blood filled his cock, leaving it fully engorged and throbbing.

Ripping his shirt off, he crossed the room and kicked his pants to the floor, pulling his boxer-briefs off at the foot of the bed.

Mary looked up, licking her lips. She locked eyes with

Tony and he knew that he was about to get some life-altering pussy.

She tossed the dildo aside, discarding it like trash. Beckoning him forward with her index finger, Tony thought he'd show her a real man.

He dove in head first, burying his face in her sex, breathing in the musky scent. He wasted no time, his tongue exploring her vagina like Lewis and Clark mapping uncharted land.

Mary's hips bucked, pushing his tongue deeper. She grabbed the back of his head, holding it in place. Her thighs squeezed the sides of his head, trapping him within her pussy.

Tony couldn't breathe, but he didn't care. Enthralled with his favorite part of human anatomy, Tony had momentarily forgotten Mary's transgressions. He loved the taste of a woman and he was eating his fill. She moaned louder and louder as Tony savored the delicacy between her legs.

She came. Hard. Tony knew by the way her body rocked in waves. She scooted back, trying to create space but Tony pulled her in and kept tonguing her.

Mary sat up and Tony sprawled out on his back. She straddled him and slowly lowered herself over his cock.

Tony hissed as her wet sex swallowed his organ to the hilt. He closed his eyes, letting her ride.

She leaned forward, whispering in his ear. "Are you ready, Tony?"

"Almost, baby, almost."

She leaned forward, raising her ass up and popped her hips up and down, sliding over his shaft. Over and Over. He felt her ass slapping against his balls and something about that sent him over the edge.

"I'm ready. Here I come," he said.

As his seed shot into Mary, she gripped him tighter. The contents of his balls erupting, his cock pulsating as the semen spurted out.

The pleasure was short-lived.

Tony felt streaks of white-hot pain tear across his chest. "What the fuck!" he said.

He opened his eyes, no longer in ecstasy. Swapping pleasure for pain. And fear.

Sitting up, but still gripping him with her unusually strong legs, Mary transformed.

Her pupils enlarged, blackness taking up the entire eyeball. A deep crimson color danced in the center of her optical orbs. Her chin elongated, the jaw cracking and the bones in her skull popping as they shifted, her entire face taking on a new shape.

Loose teeth tumbled from her mouth onto Tony's chest, making way for rows of razor-sharp teeth that looked as if they'd be at home in the mouth of a great white. Her fingers elongated as the bones grew forth from the skin, curving into vicious points. Talons.

Tony loosed a scream as those talons grabbed hold of his flesh, ripping and tearing. She opened her mouth, that hideous, grotesque oral opening now stretched to unimaginable proportions. From rabbit hole to cavern.

Not that anything about what was happening to Tony was believable. A predator by nature, it was inconceivable to him that he be turned into nothing more than prey to some creature ripped straight from Satan's worst nightmares.

She leaned forward, burying her face into his neck. Mary bit down, hard. Those horrible, impossible teeth severing the carotid artery and tearing away chunks of meat.

She gnashed her teeth, smacking her lips. Tony's

screams died down, his life essence fading fast, whimpers the only sounds escaping his lips. Wet chewing noises, and the sickening sound of his flesh tearing and being eaten were the last sounds Tony would hear as he bled out.

Even as Tony dissipated from the land of the living, Mary dined.

———

MARY HAD DEVOURED TONY. SKIN, MEAT, BONE—ALL gone. The only remaining trace of Tony stained the linens and mattress. Aside from the sheets, which Mary would simply toss overboard, Tony's luggage would be the only thing left behind. The only indication that something was awry.

Mary didn't care about that. The ship was approaching the port in Mexico and she planned to disappear long before anyone noticed the two of them hadn't returned to the ship.

They would look—of course they would. Cleanup hadn't been perfect—it never was—but there was nothing authorities could do to stop her.

Humans were nothing more than sustenance to her. If (and when) they came looking, Mary would simply have them for dinner, for she was a voracious eater.

Insatiable.

S omething ripped Ray from his slumber, long before
his alarm was due to go off. Even before he realized
he couldn't move, a feeling of dread grew in his
stomach, like he had swallowed a large stone. Eyes wide
open, he stared at the underside of Paul's bunk. The
oppressive heat alone was bad enough, but waking up
paralyzed was enough to fuck up anyone's day. Even now,
in July, the hottest month of the Iraqi summer, the heat
was poised to reach record heights. The temperature
outside of his room had not dropped below 90 degrees,
even though the sun had set hours ago. With no air conditioning or ventilation to speak of, the metal trailer used as a
dwelling was likely as hot, if not hotter, than the sweltering
Iraqi climate outside. Despite the heat, he shivered, goose-
bumps trailing along his arm. Something was triggering his
body's fight-or-flight response while also rendering him
unable to do either of those things. Clenching his teeth,
Ray strained, struggling to move his body.

He failed.

No longer afforded the luxury of locomotion, Ray

swiveled his eyeballs in their sockets. That small motion at least was still within his grasp. He scanned for either of his two roommates, hoping that one of them could help. Passed out on a beanbag chair in the center of the room, was his buddy, Mark. Paul tossed and turned on the bunk above him. Whatever malady left Ray in his current vegetative state had skipped Paul, and possibly Mark. Although Ray supposed that until Mark woke up, there was no way to know for sure. During their downtime, and in an effort to wind down and disconnect from the always on alert, patrol mindset, the three Marines had spent the past few weeks binge-watching the entire series run of *Buffy the Vampire Slayer* on DVD. During the night, the three of them had all fallen asleep without turning off either the television, or the DVD player. Still playing on the old CRT set was Ray's favorite episode, "Once more with feeling." He loved how the entire episode was done as a musical; it was genius. That the disc was still playing an episode and had not yet reverted to the main menu told Ray that he couldn't have been asleep for very long. Only an hour or two. Tops.

Sweat trickled down his spine, running along the crack of his ass before pooling on the mattress beneath him. The air inside the room changed. What the cause of the change could be, Ray did not know. The air became dense, and not from the smothering heat, but different. It took on an almost crushing weight, transforming the simple, involuntary task of breathing into a life and death struggle.

The hairs on his neck stood alert, and Ray's testicles felt as if they had ascended back into his body, nestling in the pit of his stomach. He had the distinct feeling he was being watched. It reminded him of sitting in front of the television as a child playing video games. His brother,

Mike, would try to sneak up on him, and although Mike hadn't made a peep, Ray *felt* his presence behind him.

With the memory of that feeling fresh in his mind, Ray struggled with a newfound urgency, again failing to move.

Ray refused to give up. Figuring this shit out was imperative. He was certain his life depended on it.

Staring at his feet, he focused on his toes. Maybe if he could regain control of some small part of his body, he could reclaim the rest.

Did I have a stroke? A seizure? What the fuck is going on?

It was no use. Ray was a fucking cripple, his massive frame as useless as a limp dick in a threesome. He needed to wake one of his roommates so they could call for the platoon's Navy Corpsman. He opened his mouth to speak, but the words wouldn't come.

Between his legs, a swirling black vortex formed on the mattress.

From the vortex, something rose. Inch by inch, the thing emerged from the mattress. As it continued to take shape, the black, amorphous *thing* took on physical traits. Before long, he was staring at a woman's head.

Ray's heart jackhammered in his chest, threatening to burst at any second, leaving him dead. He wouldn't even be given the honor of dying in combat. Maybe a heart attack was a better fate than living the rest of his life as a vegetable, or worse, living long enough to discover whatever the fuck was going on between his legs.

He was losing his mind. That had to be it. The pressure of combat—always wondering when you were going to be sniped, blown up by an IED, or taken out by some chicken shit with a bomb strapped to his chest—had finally cracked his mind, leaving him a few eggs short of a full basket.

Behind a veil of long, black hair, the apparition stared

at him. Black eyes set above high cheekbones. Her skin pale with death and her body covered in dirt from the grave.

Terror gripped him, and Ray once again tried to scream, but his vocal cords did not cooperate. A wet warmth spread forth from his crotch. The stench of rotting flesh commingled with his own piss, assaulting his nostrils and turning his stomach sour. The specter, now fully materialized and kneeling on his chest, grabbed at his neck with her long, dirty fingers. Each one of its fingernails felt sharp enough to easily slice through flesh like a knife through warm butter.

Ray stared in horror as she grinned, revealing a mouthful of decaying and broken teeth, set in a charred and blackened face. The phantom's skin was cracked in places, much like hardened, broken clay. Entire sections of skin were missing, revealing the muscle and bone behind it. Ray could see a few of her molars through the rot in her skin.

She really should brush her teeth better. Yep, his mind had cracked alright.

The grisly ghoul had an air of familiarity about her, and it sparked Ray's memory. He had seen this woman before and had played a role in her death.

She had been the victim of collateral damage from a mortar strike on an enemy compound. Ray was the squad leader, but the off-target round wasn't his fault. The unit's forward observer had called in the request for fire, and his squad had dropped the rounds on the coordinates provided to them. Mortar systems are indirect fire weapons which by nature meant that it was impossible for him to see his target. Your aim could be perfect, but if the observer was wrong, or the mathematics involved in converting the forward observer's surveillance into mils on a compass were wrong, the round would not go where intended.

Still struggling underneath the weight of the corpse, tears trickled down his cheeks. He felt awful about what happened. He would never intentionally harm a civilian, and her death weighed heavily upon his conscience. The night it had happened he had even considered suicide, unsure how he could live the rest of his life knowing that he was a responsible for the death of a non-combatant. Sure, he had taken lives before, but they had all been enemy combatants. Never a woman who had simply been in the wrong place at the wrong time.

She tightened her grip around his neck and pressed her lips against his. The tendons in his neck strained, bulging like ripcords, ready to split the thin layer of skin over them. The specter lost shape, deflating like a balloon losing helium. Now a shapeless mass, she forced her way through Ray's mouth, stifling his last attempt to scream.

Ray's body convulsed. His bowels emptied and shit blossomed out of his asshole, the force of the evacuation splattering the brown, watery mess along his ass cheeks and the back of his thighs.

A set of arms grabbed him by the shoulders, pinning him down.

"Dude, snap the fuck out of it," Paul said. "Did you just fucking shit yourself?"

"What? What's going on?" Ray asked.

"You had another nightmare. You were shaking the shit out of my bunk. I climbed down and you were spazzing the fuck out."

"I can't sleep, man. And when I do, I keep seeing everyone we've killed. I need to talk to Doc. Get some sleeping pills or something," Ray said.

"You need to let that shit go, man, we're in a war. Accidents happen. It wasn't your fault."

"Yeah… yeah I know."

Paul scratched his nuts. "Get in the shower and clean yourself up. It fucking stinks in here, and I'm not cleaning this shit up. After that, go see Doc, because we need your head in the game."

Both Marines let the conversation die there.

After cleaning himself and the room, Ray tossed his sheets in the trash and threw a poncho liner on his bunk. Laying on the bunk, Ray wondered what was wrong with him.

He could not sleep, while Paul had fallen back to sleep almost instantly, and Mark had somehow remained asleep for the entirety of what had happened, completely unaware of anything that had transpired.

Qrf Up!

The sun rose overhead, making good on the promise of super-heating Camp Fallujah. Ray rolled out of his bunk and put his uniform on. He picked up his hygiene kit and stepped outside, cursing the already oppressive heat. The air threatened to cook his eyeballs. It reminded him of opening an oven with your face too close to the door. He took a deep breath, choking on the fumes of flaming human shit. Every morning some poor soul had to stir a concoction of JP-8 and human feces. A foul mixture that ruined the urge to eat breakfast every day since Ray had been in country. He thanked God every morning that he had the foresight to fake a respiratory illness, exempting him from shit burning duty. Hell, knowing how bad that detail was, Ray figured he owed the doc a blowjob for exempting him.

Despite being in the middle of a war zone that stunk of death, decay, and human shit, the mornings in Iraq were peaceful, and sticking to a morning hygiene routine allowed Ray to hold on to a shred of normalcy, one that had kept him sane. Until last night.

Today, as he brushed his teeth, Ray did not feel sane. His mind played last night's nightmare on a loop. Ray told himself that it had been nothing more than a vivid dream, but there was a part of him that didn't believe it. Those dead eyes. They peered into the depths of his soul. Ray thought of how she violated his body. No, that was no dream. He had taken an innocent life, and now he would pay.

He vomited, spraying the foul contents of his stomach against the side of the trailer and in the dirt at his feet. It got on his boots and coated his uniform pants.

After the violent expulsion of what little food had been in his stomach, Ray tried to compose himself. He rubbed his eyes. The bags under his eyes had bags. He needed to sleep, but his body refused to cooperate. His squad had finished their turn on patrol and were now on rest, but they remained on Quick React Force duty. QRF was a mixed bag. There would be no scheduled missions, but being assigned QRF meant you needed to be ready to leave the wire at a moment's notice. Any rest a Marine on QRF got could be interrupted at a moment's notice. Emergency response was needed on an almost daily basis.

In order to accommodate the need for haste, the QRF team left their gear staged in the trucks according to their respective vehicle assignments. Ray was the driver of the lead vehicle, one of the most important assignments on any patrol, and after his morning hygiene was complete, the next part of his routine was a maintenance check of his vehicle. He felt out of focus, and tried to force his mind to clear the cobwebs, but the fog enveloping his brain remained. This was more than the usual morning groggi-ness. He pulled a can of Red Bull from his assault pack, cracked the tab and chugged it in one go. If he was lucky, the liquid energy boost would pump a few more hours of life into his walking corpse.

After sucking down the canned coronary, Ray grabbed his shaving kit, ready to finish his morning hygiene. He splashed water on his face and neck. Ray hated shaving, and wished he could stop. Plenty of guys could go a day or two without shaving, but no, not him. He had to be one of those hairy, sasquatch mother fuckers who had a five o'clock shadow five minutes after he put the razor down. Even in the middle of a war, Marines were required to maintain grooming standards. Some fuckwad in command that never left his tent, never had to see the horrors of war, decided that the insurgents gave a fuck if you shaved or not, and that they would assume an unshaven Marine was an unprepared Marine. You couldn't make up something that fucking stupid. Ray laughed at the absurdity of the thought. It was bullshit, but so was 90% of the shit the Marine Corps force-fed their enlistees. It was a method of indoctrination, and the Marines had developed plenty of those over the past 200-plus years of its existence.

Ray set his mirror down on the electrical box outside of his room, placing it at an angle allowing him to see his face. He grabbed his can of Barbasol and shook it, pressing the button and pumping a large puff of white foam into his hands. He worked it into a lather, raised his hands to his face, and stopped dead in his tracks.

Bruises lined his neck.

Bruises that looked like hands.

He stared, mouth agape. Ray didn't know if the rigors of war were chipping away at his mind, or if the ghost of a woman who had died a horrible death at his hands had returned for revenge. Either way, it didn't matter. Both of the options fucking terrified him.

He closed his eyes and shook his head. When he opened them, the marks were gone.

He wasn't *losing* his mind; it was long fucking gone.

Radio chatter from his hip ripped him from his trance, forcing him back to reality. Mark and Paul burst out of their room carrying their weapons.

"Let's go, Fucker! Second platoon got hit! We're up!" Paul called over his shoulder.

Ray left his hygiene kit where it lay. There was no time to clean up. Face still lathered, he snatched his rifle off the ground and sprinted toward the trucks, leaving a trail of Barbasol in his wake.

Afterword

I'd like to thank each and every person who has given this book a shot, I am forever in your debt. If you've enjoyed the book, hell even if you hated it, I'd love if you left a review over on Amazon or Goodreads, it helps with visibility of the book, and I would be forever grateful.

If not for the undying support of my wife and kids, this writing thing would be impossible for me to do. I owe Patrick Harrison III a world of thanks for his excellence in editing. He is phenomenal. Lynne Hansen is responsible for the amazing cover you hold in your hands. If you're in need of a cover, Lynne can make you a masterpiece.

I don't want to beat a dead horse, but I'm going to. Thank you all for reading this book, and for supporting my writing. You help make this possible.

John Lynch

Dec. 23, 2022

Also by John Lynch

The Warrior Retreat

About the Author

John Lynch is a Marine Corps Veteran and horror writer. He lives in Rhode Island with his wife, children, cat, and English Bulldog. You can sign up for his newsletter at john lynchbooks.substack.com and also purchase signed copies and merchandise from johnlynchbooks.bigcartel.com

 facebook.com/john.lynch.7509

 twitter.com/johnlynchbooks

 instagram.com/jlynch0341

www.ingramcontent.com/pod-product-compliance
Lightning Source LLC
Chambersburg PA
CBHW031156010826
48971CB00012B/743